Moraa Gitaa

Worlds Unknown Publishers

PROLOGUE

"Lucy! Like really now? I can't believe you've invited boys who are not from our school to the party. Karen Senior? Aren't they too old for your party?" Patricia leaned across the backseat of Lucy's parents' Range Rover Sport, and whispered into Lucy's ear so that the driver could not hear her.

Lucy ignored Patricia's question, took a sip of her branded lemon water, and said, "Stop acting so scared, Pattie. You're behaving like you've never lied to your *paroos* before."

"I'm fourteen, Lucy. Of course I've lied to my parents! But never about going to a party!"

A minute passed before anyone in the car spoke. Then Patricia turned to Lucy and gave her an inquiring look, the kind that said; *I have just remembered that you did not answer a question of mine.*

"What is it, Pattie? I'm fourteen too! *Kwani,* is there something wrong? The Karen Senior boys are just coming to my party to celebrate with us. And they do live in our complex. It's not as if they're total strangers," Lucy said. She gave Patricia a fixed look that gave the impression she was not interested in discussing the matter anymore.

Patricia bit her nails, took a long, deep and loud breath that startled Lucy, and then said, "If your *paroos* find out you held a party at night without their permission at your house, when they were away for the weekend, they'll hit the roof!"

Lucy was about to say something but Patricia cut in, leaving her with the mouth wide agape almost like her jaw was about to drop to mid-chest, "It will be worse when they know that you invited older boys they hardly even know, and then the shit will like hit the fan really, really, hard!"

"And that's why you're so nervous?" Lucy threw back. She leaned towards Patricia as if the trouble was already there, and she was meeting it head-on.

"No. I just think that you should call your *paroos* and tell them about the party. It might then be easier for me to tell mine too, this being my first all-night party." Patricia's suggestion was met with total silence from Lucy.

Shortly, Lucy looked at Patricia. "We are so used to our age-mates and fellow boy students at Karen Preparatory. I think hot, new, older boys, from a different school like Karen Senior School will make the party awesome and much cooler." Lucy stared at Patricia, begging with her eyes as if to say that they had talked enough about it, and there was no need to continue the discussion.

"Whatever!" Patricia responded but she was still not too sure if Lucy's idea was so cool after all. Lucy encouraged Patricia, convincing her that there was nothing wrong with having the boys attend the party. Lucy's words calmed and psyched Patricia up for the party. To Lucy, this night was a celebration of what they had achieved in life so far; that of clearing primary school, and looking forward to joining high school. None of them, however, could predict that the night would mark the beginning of something too dark for neither themselves, nor their parents to handle.

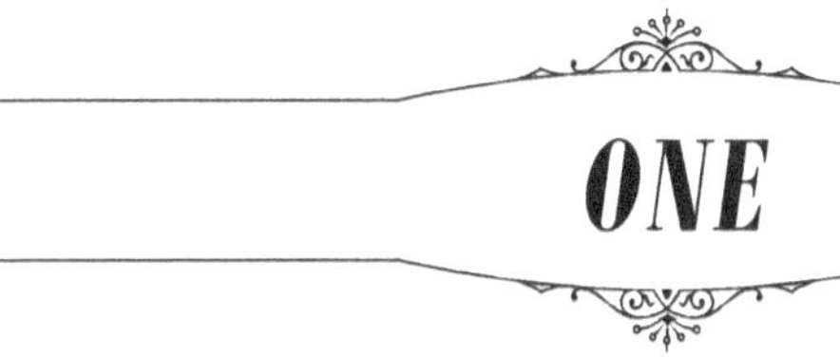

ONE

There was no showy sign announcing the five-star Angels of Mercy Girl's Crisis Centre. Just a high, black steel gate, with a discreet tiny bronze nameplate expensively etched into the stone pillars flanking the driveway in the leafy suburb. The perimeter wall surrounding the property had atop it, electric wire fencing running round it.

Patricia's mother stretched her hand out of the open front passenger seat window, and pressed a button on the stone pillar. A voice from a sort of intercom on the pillar, asked her to confirm her name and appointment time, which she did. The gate then swung open automatically, and closed behind them. Patricia's father slowed down as he steered the car, following the winding cobble-stoned driveway, lined with jacaranda trees in full purple bloom, and flame trees with big bright orange flowers. A couple of bumps slowed them down further. Patricia seated in the backseat, surveyed the impeccable grounds – her new home for the next couple of weeks. Workmen were busy laying a new landscape. A gardener in green overalls, raking dry leaves into heaps raised his hand in greeting. Patricia's parents waved back at the gardener but their daughter looked away, not bothering to wave back. Patricia's eyes were more vacant than ever. Throughout the journey, Patricia's face was fixed in a frown. Her stubborn lips completed the perfect picture of a rebellious face. If Lucy or Vera, her two best friends were here, they would have said that if someone looked closely at Patricia, he or she would see fumes of furious smoke blow out of Patricia's eyes and ears. Moments later, the three were standing at the flag-stoned courtyard, and were ushered into the building by the security guard. A receptionist welcomed them.

Despite the doctors having recommended the therapy at this place, Patricia took it as only one piece in the long chain of conspiracies, that her parents had created to avoid having her close to them ever since her terrible ordeal.

Within an hour, Patricia had been checked in, and her parents had left. A middle-aged woman, with a head full of hair in a huge natural afro, introduced herself as Madam Christine, the head nurse.

"Why are you doing this?" Patricia asked the head nurse ransacking her bags. The head nurse replied, "We explained to you and your parents when you were checked in, that every patient's luggage has to be inspected." Patricia did not remember having been party to such a conversation. The nurse insisted that Patricia could not have her hair drier because it could be used as a weapon in a bath full of water to harm herself, and therefore dangerous. Patricia watched, her upper lip curled in anger, as the nurse delicately transferred her manicure sets into a tray. The nurse said in a softer voice, "We shall only bring you things that you're allowed to have in your room, until you finish your therapy." Patricia her voice petulant, snapped, *"Holy shit! What do you mean allowed?"*

"It's for your own safety and protection, Patricia," the nurse answered. "We search and go through and take everything that might be deemed dangerous, and raise an inventory for your stuff in our computer system."

The nurse went on explaining to her the other procedures, but Patricia was no longer listening. She held her waist and softly tapped her right foot—which was slightly ahead of the left one—on the floor. Patricia secretly studied the nurse's pretty face as she waited for her to finish. When the nurse noticed Patricia's face twitching with anger, she added, "We will return all your items once you finish the therapy." When that did not result in any response of relief from Patricia, the nurse smiled for the first time and told Patricia, her voice much softer than before, "If you need any of what we have taken today, all you have to do is come to one of us, and we shall even come and help you do nails, or dry your dreadlocks once you've washed them."

"Okay! Okay! I get it!" Patricia's voice bordered on shouting, as the head nurse left the room. Patricia kicked off her sneakers, and then stretched out on the bed.

Patricia imagined how long her stay there would last, and what it would be like. The restrictions on what items to keep in her room, made her realize that her freedom was now curtailed, and maybe even gone forever. *If only I had not attended that party. But how could I not?* She asked herself. First, her vivacious spirit had been broken, then her freedom was taken away, and then she could no longer talk to her parents as she had done before. Patricia could not believe that, the same father who had now become silent and not ready to talk about what she had gone through that night, was the same one who had always been talkative and lively. She could not imagine that he was the same father who used to take his family on vacations at the beach down coast in Mombasa and Watamu. One such happy family time was when they went to the five-star, Blue Bay Beach Resort in Watamu, along the coast of Kenya.

"Pattie! Come on now! This is a father-daughter bonding moment. Do you need to look at your phone all the time? Why on earth can't you kids just live in the moment?" Mr Kwela's voice was exasperated.

"*Awww*…Dad! If I don't look at my phone, like all the time, how then does one IG such moments for posterity?" Patricia pouted her peach-balmed lips, and snuggled closer to her father, holding aloft the selfie stick with her iPhone perched high on it and snapped a couple of selfies. She smiled at the perfect photographs showing her in a brand new purple and flowery designer bikini. "Daddy, just a moment while I post this on IG and share on Snapchat!"

"Pattie, be careful. Remember what we've talked about before. Don't share your photos all over the internet, with just about anybody on social media." But Patricia was only half listening. Her attention was already divided between admiring her approaching beautiful mother, and uploading the photos online. "There are many dangerous characters out there who can do harmful things with your photos and images," her father added.

"Yes, Dad. And thanks! But you know I'm always very careful. *Ama*?" Patricia said, and then as if an afterthought added, "I only share with friends like Vera and Lucy." Patricia's best friends, Vera and Lucy, were both fourteen like her.

"Good for you, my girl!" her father said.

Patricia could not take her eyes of her mother who was walking over to join them at the poolside, to inform them she was going shopping in Malindi, a ten-minute drive away.

Mrs Kwela looked like she'd just stepped out of the cover of Vogue with a stunning flowery Zara sundress, the latest Marc Jacobs handbag on her arm, Dior stunners shading her eyes from the brilliant coastal sun. A Patek Phillipe watch with diamonds adorned her slender wrist and the deliciously fragrant smell of her favorite Calvin Klein's latest perfume Euphoria wafted off her. She dug into her Louis Vuitton clutch, and added more Lancome nude shade lip-gloss to her already perfect lips.

A sudden thumping on one wall brought Patricia back from her memories and to the present moment, in her room at Angels of Mercy Girl's Crisis Centre.

A couple of hours had gone by since Patricia arrived, yet she'd not changed out of her clothes. She had not even taken a bath but was still resting, stretched out on her bed. She drew her knees to her chest, and using her palms, covered each ear. The slamming on the wall continued. The thumping penetrated Patricia's covered ears. *What kind of place was this?* She asked herself. *First, the nurse had confiscated my stuff, now that deafening sound from the room next to mine? Have I been duped and dumped in a home for mad people?* The continued thumping interrupted her train of thought. Patricia slid off the bed, slipped her feet into a pair of fluffy, pink bathroom sandals, and stepped onto the polished wooden fishbone parquet floor.

She walked to the door and opened it, careful not to run into danger, for all she could think of now, was colliding with an insane person running up and down the corridor. Her heart began to race as she took a look to the right, left, then back right up the corridor.

She took a few tiny, hesitant steps towards the room adjacent to hers, to the left, where the slamming sound was coming from. She first squinted, then opened and closed her eyes, repeating the exercise until her eyes got used to the bright fluorescent corridor lights which had come on a few minutes earlier. She noticed a beam of light shining from under a door, and guessed that the sounds were most probably coming from that room. The corridor was deserted but the thumping sounds next door continued without stopping. Patricia's chest heaved in panic.

She tiptoed toward the sounds, her body pressed against the cold concrete wall. She swallowed hard, her heartbeat pulsating in her ears. *Maybe I should go back to my room,* she thought, but her curious feet led her towards the room. After several moments of inching along the wall, Patricia peeked into the open door. Inside, she spotted a dark, slender girl, tearing the room apart. The girl pulled out drawers and emptied the wardrobe, throwing clothes to the polished, wooden floor. Every minute the girl interchanged the hurling of items, with hitting the wall with her right foot in kick-boxing style. *So that was the thumping sound,* Patricia thought, but just as she was about to turn and creep back to her room unnoticed, the girl turned around and saw her.

"Are you spying on me, you stupid girl?" she asked, her eyes big like marbles, the dark iris almost disappearing into the whites, darted from side to side wildly. The girl bunched her fists into balls as if getting ready for a fight with Patricia.

"*Uhhhh?*" was all that Patricia said, caught off-guard and having not much time to think. Then she added in fear, her voice wobbly, "No, I'm not spying on you! I was wondering if you needed any help."

Patricia wished someone could appear from the corridor as she could use any help, but hearing no footfalls, imagined the violent girl advancing on her. Was the girl mad? Had her parents brought Patricia here, because they thought her condition was similar? Patricia could hear her heart throbbing and beating louder against her chest. To her relief, the girl had already lost interest in her, and was back to kicking the wall and wrecking her room.

Thankfully, at that minute, the head nurse Madam Christine came in, accompanied by an older woman who was dressed like a doctor. The nurse had now tied her big fro, using a purple pony-band into a bun on top of her head. The older woman was in a white, knee-length laboratory coat, with a silver stethoscope hung around her neck. Her round face bore a kindly expression between a worried frown and a faint smile.

"What is wrong?" the older woman gently asked the girl.

"I'm looking for my babies! My two babies! Where have my twins gone?" the girl replied between sobs, her voice anxious and agitated. Her shoulders heaved and her hands trembled.

Patricia saw the doctor put on gloves and pull out a syringe from the right pocket of the overcoat, after the nurse had helped lay the girl on the bed. Patricia made a swift U-turn.

Patricia turned and tiptoed to the corridor, thinking that the doctor might come for her too. In the corridor, Patricia leant on the wall and shook her head in relief, making her shoulder-length dreadlocks dance crazily in the process. She had only taken a couple of steps towards her room, when she missed colliding headlong into another girl by an inch.

TWO

The girl Patricia had nearly bumped into stood there, unperturbed. She trained her eyes on Patricia's face and noticed the strain on her face. They were the same height such that even as the girl stole glances at Patricia's dreadlocks, she did it with much ease without diverting Patricia's attention. After what seemed like an eternity, she broke the silence, her voice carrying a beautiful low timbre punctuated with an accent Patricia found interesting. "Hello. My name is Halkano," the girl said. Patricia said nothing in response. Her silence did not stop the girl's cheerfulness. Halkano stretched her hand to supplement the greeting and continued, "Halkano is a Borana name. It means I was born at night."

A brief smile escaped Patricia's lips. She wondered, what a strange greeting.

"I come from Marsabit County in northern Kenya. What's your name?" Halkano was not giving up on striking a conversation, and neither did Patricia's silence discourage her from trying.

"Hi, Halkano. I'm Patricia. My friends call me Pattie." She shook Halkano's still outstretched hand.

"Patricia. What does it mean?" Halkano asked.

Patricia's smile returned, this time wider. *This girl sure was strange.* "Nothing. It's just an English name," she said.

"But names have meanings," Halkano pressed on. "I'm Muslim by the way." Patricia began to picture the kind of strange girls she was going to have to live with here. First, a girl tearing her room apart, saying she was looking for her two babies, and now this one who could not stop talking, saying her name meant she was born at night!

The talkative girl whose speech had a sort of weightless cadence, like a slow lullaby song, continued, "I'm Halkano Abaduba. Sometimes my brother and sister call me Halkii in short. Abaduba is my father's name."

Patricia sighed. Her eyes remained transfixed on the ground. She was dumbfounded by each continued strange utterance that came from Halkano. Her suspicions about this place being a home for the mad and strange, were being proved right with each passing moment.

Halkano continued, "My Baba was named Abaduba, because his father died while his mother was giving birth to him. It means, 'After the Father'. So Abaduba he became. My elder brother is named Galgalo, because he was born in the afternoon. And our younger sister is Guyo for she was born during the day. Our Mama is Gadana because she was born during migration!"

Patricia did not know whether to smile at this girl, laugh at all the funny things Halkano was saying, or sympathize with herself at being brought here. Instead, she shrugged, dropped her head, and said, "Cool. Whatever. I'm a Christian. Catholic. We live here in Nairobi in Karen. My parents are James and June Kwela. So I'm Patricia Kwela. I'm an only child. I don't have any siblings." All Patricia now wanted was to get back to her room, away from anyone else.

Halkano's eyes enlarged at Patricia's statements, and especially noticed it when she said cool and whatever, in every other sentence. Patricia wondered; *was Halkano finding her words strange?*

Patricia then also stared at Halkano. The other girl had a delicate face that gave an example of what a sculptor who specialized in crafting African beauty would have chiselled. Although her manner of speaking was different, the strange girl was beautiful. The kind of African beauty Patricia saw only in high-end fashion magazines. The ones her mom bought, like *Couture Africa*, *Vanity Fair*, and *Vogue*. Halkano's head was shaven smooth and shiny with a strange smelling oil. Her skin was smooth, dark, and she had long fine hands. A tiny silver nose-ring adorned the right side of her nose.

Then all of a sudden, Halkano reached over and touched Patricia's shoulder-length dreadlocks, "Your school allows you to have these?" she asked Patricia.

"Yeah. It's a private school and they allow us any hairstyle. Our school rules aren't too strict," Patricia replied.

"But isn't that why schools have rules? To be strict?" the curious Halkano went on.

Patricia shrugged and again said, "Whatever."

As the two continued to converse, Patricia began to sense that Halkano was just a curious girl. Moments later, they walked together for a short while along the corridor. Halkano's room was further down the hallway, where they parted ways.

By the time Patricia slipped back into her room, she felt a little relieved that in Halkano she might find a friend in this strange place.

The following day in the evening, during group therapy session, Halkano noticed Patricia from last evening. She went and sat beside her. In the natural light penetrating through the wide, open windows, Patricia could see Halkano's large brown eyes that stood on her narrow face. All the girls in the session were seated in a circle. In the middle, Patricia noticed an empty chair.

"What is it with the empty chair?" Patricia wondered aloud, addressing the question to no one in particular.

"I've been here a few days already. Just wait and see. The counsellor does this every two or so days," Halkano whispered to her, revealing perfect white teeth. Halkano had today covered her head in a beautiful, colourful, silk *hijab*. The door to the room opened, and a short, petite lady in black, flat, baby-doll pumps, stepped into the room, her friendly smile announcing her presence more than her grey pant-suit did. She closed the door behind her, making the circle of girls in the centre of the room even more conspicuous.

"Hello, girls. My name is Jane. I'm the counsellor for the group therapy sessions," she said while looking at Patricia and welcoming her with a gracious smile. "Because we have a new member this evening, I'll start this session by going around the room in brief introductions. Tell us your name and the reason why you are here at Angels of Mercy. Let's go round starting to my left here," She pointed at a girl who had a timid look on her face.

Patricia's heart was racing wildly, knowing she would be third in line to introduce herself. She decided to listen to the first two girls and then follow from their example.

"Hi. I'm Susan. I miscarried my twin babies, and I've been missing them ever since then." Patricia remembered the girl who she had seen messing up her room. Today the girl appeared much calmer.

"Hello. My name is Peris and I was recently diagnosed with Bipolar. The doctor told my parents that it is a fairly new condition for many people, and that I needed to be helped into living with it. I'm here to learn how to cope living with it."

When the second girl finished, Patricia felt all eyes in the room settle on her. Even though two girls had already introduced themselves, none had said anything that inched any closer to her situation. She still was unsure of what to say. Her eyes swept across the room and settled on the counsellor. Jane slowly nodded, as if telling her to not fear.

"Hi. I'm—I'm Patricia," she stammered and fell silent.

"Go on, Patricia. Tell us why you're here if you feel strong enough, and ready to share. All of us will be doing the same," Jane prompted, smiling to encourage her. Patricia turned to look at Halkano, who nodded at her too like Jane the counsellor.

"I-I don't know," Patricia said and dropped her eyes then continued, "I-I went through a terrible ordeal and started having suicidal thoughts. I guess that's why my doctor felt I should be here." *Please, please, can you move on to the next person,* Patricia begged silently in her heart.

"Well done, Patricia! Do feel welcome. You'll soon be at home here at Angels of Mercy and start sharing more about your ordeal. Here we take it slow, one day at a time. Next!"

"Good evening. I'm Halkano. I was forced out of school and married off by my father. As a result I suffered damage to my private parts. I'm here so I can heal."

Patricia was amazed and moved, by how easily Halkano found it to talk about her experience. Could it be because she had been here for longer? Would she too find it easy to talk about her ordeal in the coming days? She hoped so. Patricia began to think that perhaps the place was not as dangerous as she first thought. However, she could not judge just yet. She would have to wait and see.

"Halkano, do you want to try as we agreed, using the word for what you went through? It will be helpful to your healing if you start saying it out loud." The counsellor paused, looking at Halkano.

"Okay. Yes, Madam Jane. I was raped and I'm here to learn how to come to terms with it." At this, Patricia found conviction that finally, there would be someone who could understand what she had gone through.

After the introductions were over, Jane addressed Patricia directly. "Patricia," she began, "you are new to this group therapy, so I'll explain to you in brief what the sessions entail. This here is our healing circle, and it's a safe space where you're welcome. You heal at your own pace, taking one day at a time, and there is no judgement whatsoever. The purpose of these circle meetings is to have more time for group therapy. We set aside one hour for this session because we've found out that the extra half hour unlike the morning session, allows us time to connect and go deeper into our thoughts."

"The chair represents someone or something you would like to address," Jane explained, "Maybe it's someone you are mad at. Or something that has caused you pain, deep anguish, and maybe suffering. Only you alone can address what this chair represents to you. Just remember there is no right or wrong way to react to rape, or any form of sexual assault. That is why it is important to get support and counselling. There is no set way to feel. You are allowed to be sad, angry, and defensive. And it's also okay to want to be alone, and not want to talk." Jane concluded her statement, by telling Patricia that it was okay to be depressed. Jane added, "At the moment you are fragile and vulnerable. What you are going through are emotions I call the three S's namely shame, silence and survivor's guilt. But slowly but surely you shall overcome." In these words, Patricia found comfort, but in her mind flashed three faces that she was trying to forget from that horrible night of the party. She imagined the three squeezed onto the seat the counsellor was talking about, in the centre of the circle.

"Five minutes are up," the counsellor announced, "Everyone in Team B, please get up and move to the right, and sit with a new partner from Team A." She had made a point of reminding the girls the rules of the exercise, because some of the girls liked sticking with friends they had made. "Don't forget the rules. Team A stays put this time around and only Team B members shift partners around the room."

It had now been several days.

"I really don't like this group therapy thingy," Patricia one day complained while talking to Halkano.

"Why?" Halkano asked.

Instead of answering her question, Patricia added another sentiment, "I prefer the one on one sessions with Dr Bilal instead."

However, in the group therapy, Patricia had learnt that the patients at the clinic were girls her age, or a little older, who had undergone traumatic experiences through the narrations that the girls gave. Others were there to adapt to conditions they had, and learn to cope living with them, like Borderline Personality Disorder shortened to BPD, Schizophrenia, and also Bipolar like Peris had shared on that first day. Yet others refused to talk. On that first day, Patricia had learnt that the girl next door to her room, whom she had found ripping her room apart the day before, was called Susan and was sixteen. Patricia was replaying the events of the group therapy in her mind. *Some girls refuse to speak at times. Others are speaking of terrible things that had happened to them.* It was something she found they had in common because, even though their experiences were different, reality had remained mysterious. At least in this facility, Patricia felt she could find people willing to understand what she underwent that night at Lucy's party. However, she was yet to understand why her parents were indifferent to her situation after that night. Each time she recalled how she had to do something stupid, whenever she needed to get her parents' attention, or tell them how she felt, tears stung her eyelids, and turned into rivulets that streamed down her cheeks. She imagined then that her parents were the ones now seated in the chair in the middle of the circle. Her mind went back to one such moment...

THREE

Patricia stared at the glistening, tiny but sharp surgical razor blade. *Everyone at school knows what happened to me. Most of them are my neighbours and I can't face them.* Patricia had sneaked the new, shiny, and thin blade off the nurse's tray of surgical syringes and equipment. *Is it possible for this tiny razor to end a human life? Two quick slashes on my wrists and the pain I feel in my heart will bleed away. I have seen such scenes countless times in the movies.* However much Patricia wanted to bring her suffering to an end, the thought of the painful slash of the blade, made her wonder if the solution had to be as painful as what she went through on the night of the party.

Before her ordeal, Patricia had watched a YouTube video—in which a teenage girl, a victim of cyber-bullying in America, live-streamed her suicide to the world when she hanged herself in the bedroom wardrobe—the clip had gone viral. Patricia had watched the clip over and over again before YouTube pulled it down. Her father later pointed out that YouTube pulled the video because of humanitarian reasons, and the privacy of the victim's family. The hanging-suicide looked painful. Was there a less painful method to kill oneself? Patricia moved her gaze from the thin metal blade she had left on the bathroom shelf, above the silver towel rail, and shifted her gaze to the sleeping pills.

Would she die if she took all those dozens of pills at once, just like she'd also seen in the movies? Patricia closed the plastic shower curtain, removed her bathrobe and dropped it to the tiled floor. She climbed into the porcelain bathtub, which was already full of warm water and turned off the tap. Would it be better and less painful for her parents, if they were told she accidentally drowned in the bathtub, after overdosing on the pills? But Patricia knew they would not buy that, because she was a champion swimmer on their school swim team.

...Patricia woke up from her afternoon nap, screaming and sweating. It was the same nightmare again—her committing suicide to escape the misery. How had she ended up like this? Her life twisted, and her sleeping moments full of plans to end her life by slicing her wrists, then overdosing on pills, and letting herself drown in a hospital bathtub? Was killing herself the only way out of the pain she was in, which her parents didn't seem to understand? She got up from the bed and went into the bathroom. *Calm down, Pattie. Calm down, girl*, she repeated to herself over and over again.

Patricia gently touched her lower abdomen and winced at the pain. Her right upper arm also still felt sore from the IV plastic tubing the nurse had removed that morning. She still couldn't walk properly but wanted to go home. At the Karen Hospital, she felt sad and her mind kept going back to that night. *Could all this have been avoided, if I had not gone to the party? What did my friends think about what happened?* She imagined that perhaps an environment away from the hospital would be better.

Just the previous night another girl had been checked into the room next to hers, and all Patricia could hear was sobbing for hours from next door. Patricia had listened keenly to the footfalls and constant melody of the shoes tapping on the floor as the nurses and doctors went in and out of the room several times. It was the same thing in her room, the night she was rushed there. Lucy and Vera's fading voices had been replaced with that of nurses talking and crowding her bed. Her eyes had opened and closed intermittently. Each time an eye opened, a figure in a long, white overcoat was standing over her. And then the figure would leave, and taps of the feet against the tiled floor fading. Then they would return to perform more tests and procedures on her. She was exhausted and wondered when all of it would come to an end. But the nurses and doctors had explained that all the tests and examinations were necessary. They had told her that the body examination was for marks, bruises and treatment of injuries. Then they explained that samples of blood, urine, including vaginal and anal fluids, would also be taken for laboratory tests. The nurse had explained that an HIV test would also be done and if she was negative, she would be given anti-retroviral drugs to prevent HIV infection. And that if she tested positive, she would be referred for care and treatment, and would also receive drugs to prevent sexually transmitted diseases, and receive counselling. Patricia was startled by all this information and the fact that she would also be tested for pregnancy, and if it turned out negative, she would be given emergency contraceptive pills to prevent pregnancy. A part of Patricia was relieved though with the all the tests, because she couldn't remember if her rapists had used condoms or not.

"Baby," Patricia's mother said from the seat beside the bed. "I'm still trying to understand why you sneaked out that night. Why didn't you call your father or me to pick you from the party after you felt uncomfortable when those older boys crashed the party?"

"Mom," Patricia answered wearily, "I just got permission to be discharged and I'm exhausted. Can we not start this conversation right now, please? So like always by you, I didn't do the right thing? Sorry to disappoint you once again, Mom!"

"Well, you did go to the party without our permission. And I still don't get why you didn't call us, yet you had your phone. Baby, Dad and I do always tell you that choices have consequences!"

"Thanks, Mom! This is making me feel much better," Patricia replied sarcastically, expecting to have her mother drop the discussion.

"Well, I for one think that—" her mother continued, ignoring the sarcasm. She smoothed the skirt of her skirt-suit with nervous hands.

"Mom. Drop it!" Patricia shouted.

A moment later, Patricia looked up at her mother. Something didn't feel right. "Mom, where's Dad?"

"Baby, he wanted to come but was busy." Mrs June Kwela flinched, waiting for her daughter's response. Her eyes lifted and moved in unison with her lips, to feign a smile.

"Whatever! *Si* you just stop trying to cover up for him, please. We both know he pretends like I wasn't raped. Like it never happened at all!" Patricia's voice cracked. She tried to force the tears choking her back down her throat.

"Pattie baby, you know Daddy would have liked to be here if he was able to, but he was held up in a meeting," her mother tried again.

"Mom, don't make excuses for him, okay?" Patricia's voice rose. "Why are you always doing this? Taking his side? He would have been here if he was able to? So what happened?"

Patricia yelled, not caring about who might hear her. Mrs Kwela stretched her hand to reach her daughter, but Patricia raised hers in an abrupt and sudden movement to stop her, and said, "Something more important came up, than picking his gang-raped daughter from the hospital, after she'd been discharged? He's always busy! Mom, you're also a busy land surveyor consultant and you're here, but my busy investment management professional of a father couldn't make it!"

Mrs Kwela grimaced and cringed. She nervously motioned to Patricia, moving her hands up and down, silently signalling her to lower her voice. "What, Mom? You don't want me embarrassing you?"

"Pattie, please keep your voice down. I know you're upset, baby," her mother almost begged.

"I'm not upset, Mom. I was raped! And I'm so tired of you covering up for Dad when he has excuses not to come and see me! This whole *he would have liked to be here* thingy is so silly and freaking stupid!" Patricia stood up from the bed.

"Watch your language, Pattie," Mrs Kwela warned. Her upper lip curled into a distasteful line, the crow's feet at the corners of her eyes crinkled and crowded together in worry.

"Oh, for heaven's sake give it up, Mom! Look around you and wake up from your fantasy world. Go to the room next to mine, and you'll find a girl like me who's also been raped. *Raped! Raped!* Do you understand? You think anyone around here cares about language?" Pattie tried to mimic her mother's conciliatory tone.

"Young lady, I'm still your mother and the way you're talking to me is bothering me! And I'm not making excuses for your father over this issue," her mother said in finality.

"Dad's had one big hangover of denial ever since I was raped! As if it never happened and the two times he's visited me here in hospital, he refuses to talk about it. It's the unspoken of topic!"

"Come here, baby." Her mother stood up and stretched out her hands once more. Mrs Kwela felt that it was a losing battle she was fighting.

"No, you don't, Mom! Don't you dare baby me, ever again!" Patricia shouted hysterically. She sidestepped her mother's outstretched hands, and brushed past her, running into the bathroom, thankful it was a private room from which no one could hear her sobbing. For a moment Patricia looked at the poster on the wall, which explained steps to take when a person had been raped. Part of the poster said in bulleted form; GO TO the nearest hospital or police station as soon as possible, within 72 hours after the rape. DO NOT wash or clean any part of your body, or comb your hair. DO NOT destroy, change, lose or wash your clothes. WRAP THEM in a non-polythene paper such as a khaki bag or in clean cotton clothes. DO NOT put the clothes in a plastic or polythene bag or in a newspaper. TAKE THE clothes to the hospital with you, and let the health care provider examine them. DO NOT change anything at the crime scene.

The poster went on to explain the tests that would be conducted on the victim at the hospital, and the role of the police. Patricia sighed deeply. She knew she was lucky that Lucy's adult neighbours had known to do all of the above, before rushing her to the hospital. She felt encouraged when she read again the last line of the poster: Remember that it is NOT your fault! It is the person who raped you who is wrong. DO NOT FEEL GUILTY. DO NOT BE ASHAMED. ALWAYS REMEMBER, YOU ARE NOT TO BLAME. IT WAS NOT YOUR FAULT. YOU ARE THE VICTIM. YOUR ABUSER IS THE ONE WHO COMMITTED A CRIME AGAINST YOU. DO NOT BLAME YOURSELF.

FOUR

At the Karen Mall, the automatic glass doors slid open when Mrs Kwela, Patricia, and her friends Vera and Lucy, neared the entrance. Vera as usual, was accompanied by Lulu, her pet dog, a tiny, white, fluffy poodle. Patricia said unlike Vera, she was a cat-person and had told her parents she too wanted a pet, and her choice was a cat. They had promised her they will go and adopt one from the Kenya Society for the Protection and Care of Animals, the KSPCA's place in Karen, just a few metres from their home, on Langata road opposite Hillcrest School.

Immediately they were inside the mall, the girls of course turned on the GPS locations on their phones, and snapped a group selfie. It was a Saturday evening, two weeks after Patricia's discharge from Karen Hospital, and her mother had offered to treat the girls to a girl's day out and movie. It was the premiere of the re-made *Lion King*, and the IMAX screening auditorium was full. The girls were excited because apart from the movie being one of their favorite, the soundtrack by American singer Beyoncé, featured various African artists. It was so cool and awesome when Beyoncé sang in Kiswahili, '*Uishi kwa muda mrefu Mfalme*', meaning 'Long live the King.' Patricia always imagined the movie being shot on location at the Masai Mara National Reserve, where she had been many times with her parents, and seen a pride of lions. She would visualize the tense moment when a real life Rafiki the shaman baboon, held Mufasa the father Lion's little son Simba, high up on Pride Rock over the cliff, while the horrible Scar, schemed and plotted to be King!

After the movie, they bought ice-cream and delicious Fro-Yo—as the girls called the frozen yoghurt in short—at Yoghurt Planet. It was only just past nine and because the mall closed at midnight, they decided to have Chinese for dinner at their favorite restaurant in the mall before shopping. They went to the bookstore and bought several Young Adult fiction novellas, then went shopping at one of the designer outlets. Vera and Lucy picked several beautiful skirts and blouses. Patricia had thrown into her pull-trolley, a pair of trendy boot-cut jeans, torn at the knees, and tee-shirts.

"Pattie," her mother snapped, throwing a cursory side-glance at the stuff in Patricia's trolley, "Why don't you for once pick even one skirt? Look at the lovely dresses your friends have selected," her eyes shifted to Vera and Lucy, "You don't need more jeans. You actually have some new ones in your wardrobe that you've not even worn. Please my dear, just pick a dress or skirt today!"

"Whatever, Mom!" Patricia said. "But there are no dresses or skirts I like here." She walked aimlessly around the large departmental store, touching dresses and blouses without picking any to try in the changing room. Patricia pouted and sulked. She was furious with her mother for calling her out in front of her friends, like she did not know what she was doing. She was going to show her!

At the make-up display, Patricia smiling, picked an expensive designer lip-gloss, and slipped it into her jeans pocket. Then, she quickly followed her mother and friends to the checkout counter. Mrs Kwela paid for everything they had bought using her credit card, which the cashiers swiped on the card-reader which was beside the Point-of-Sale system. By the time they were done and leaving the store, the rope handles on the shopping bags were digging into Patricia's hands but she didn't mind. Something bigger was about to happen. It was time for a showdown with Mom!

At the entrance as they walked out—Mrs Kwela, Lucy, and Vera already on the other side—walked out effortlessly, but as Patricia drifted through the scanner, she set off a red light and series of beeps at the electronic archway. The two security guards rushed towards her, their hands held up, warning her not to proceed farther. Patricia backed away.

Mrs Kwela came back to the main electronic archway. "Is there a problem, officer? This is my daughter."

"Sorry, Madam. Something you haven't paid for is setting off the scanner's alarm," the security guard said, as another guard appeared at his other side.

"But I paid for everything," Mrs Kwela attempted again, pulling out the receipts from her handbag to show the guards. All the bags were again passed through the scanner and the beeping was silent. The four were requested to pass through again. When Mrs Kwela, Lucy, and Vera passed through, no alarm sounded. However, when it was Patricia's turn to pass through a second time, the red light came on again and the automatic beeper went off loudly. Mrs Kwela told Patricia to remove her silver earrings of a pair of dolphins in a synchronized dive. The three girls had all emptied their tiny leather backpacks which had iPads, iPhones, house keys, and several coins, onto a plastic tray before passing through, and so Mrs Kwela thought it was the earrings which set off the scanner. Patricia did as her mother asked, removed the dolphin earrings and walked through the metal detector again. The beeping went off for a third time.

One of the female guards reached for a body scanning hand-held electronic device, and waved it up and down the length of Patricia's body, then patted her down. She felt something in Patricia's right jeans pockets and pulled it out. It was the lip-gloss Patricia had nicked at the make-up counter.

Vera and Lucy, with jaws almost dropping to the ground, unable to move, stood still with surprise. They fixed their shocked gaze on Patricia.

Vera, as if regaining her composure, ran her hands over her soft, shiny, relaxed dark hair tied at the back with a velvet maroon pony band. Then she cuddled her poodle Lulu closer, looked at her friends, then rolled her eyes dramatically until they almost disappeared into the back of her skull, and said in disgust "Patricia! Like really, girl? Did you just steal lip-gloss? Y'all this is so like gross!"

Lucy, with an angry frown covering her tiny face, removed her wireless headphones and hung them around her neck. Then she also quipped, "Bestie, *si* you're just so dramatic? All this major drama just for some lip-gloss! If your mom was not here, you would end up in mall jail!" She too did a dramatic eye-roll.

Mrs Kwela slapped her hands together multiple times in shock, and said, "Patricia! Since when did you develop itchy and sticky fingers? Why on earth are you shoplifting?"

Patricia pouted her lips defiantly, staring at her mother in silence. The guards called the departmental store's manager.

"Lucy and Vera, could you please wait in the car?" Mrs Kwela turned to Patricia, "Walk with me!" They marched behind the manager to a room where a man and a woman operator, sat before several large screens mounted on the wall. They viewed the CCTV footage from earlier on, and saw Patricia sneaking the lip-gloss into her pocket.

Mrs Kwela and Patricia accompanied the manager back to his office. He asked them to be seated. They sat on the far end of his large desk.

"Young girl," the manager asked as if he and Patricia were good friends, "Do you understand what this means for you and your mother?"

Silence.

"Patricia!" Mrs Kwela shouted, her face shining with embarrassment in the bright light of the room.

Patricia remained silent.

The manager and Patricia's mother exchanged resigned looks.

"Do you understand the consequences of this, young girl?" the manager addressed Patricia.

Silence.

"Do you know that it is illegal and you can go to jail for this?"

Silence.

"Why did you do it?"

The manager asked Patricia to go outside and leave them alone for a short moment.

"Look, Mrs Kwela," he said, "Considering the cordial relationship you have had with our store in the past, and that you are regulars here, I will let this go today."

Mrs Kwela heaved a long sigh of relief, stood up and said, "Thank you so much. I really appreciate your understanding. I assure you this will not happen again."

They got into Mrs Kwela's Porsche Cayenne and belted up. On the drive back to Karen, in the passenger front seat, Patricia was silent but kept throwing side-eyes at her mother. Lucy and Vera were also quiet in the back seat. Lulu the poodle, as if understanding the grave situation, did not bark even a tiny bit. They drove past Bomas of Kenya, down Mamba Village the crocodile farm, and off Langata Road. Patricia shrank further back into her seat, the way she did every time they passed the Karen Hospital along Karen-Langata Road, for it reminded her of the night she was rushed there after being raped.

Mrs Kwela was trying hard to appear stern but in her heart she was disturbed. She could sense her daughter's side-glances, and resisted giving her a harsh side-eye in response. After a short while, Mrs Kwela did steal a quick glance at her daughter, and found Patricia deep in thought. Mrs Kwela's own thoughts then turned inwards to her worries… *There is something terrifying about when your kid becomes a teenager, and starts keeping secrets because she feels she now has a mind of her own that you can no longer read! Then starts sneaking out for parties and she pulls away from you, making it harder to protect her, to keep her safe. But the thing is, that's all normal and natural and I had to let it happen…but this was until the horrible rape, which was terrible and traumatizing, and now I don't know how to deal with it, nor how to talk to her about it. The reason she's acting out like this, by shoplifting, which is so unlike her! And to make matters worse the Google and internet searches she has been making online, about suicides and methods of killing oneself like the razor blade and over-dosing search. But how to even bring this up without your daughter feeling that you are snooping on her, because she as yet doesn't know how to delete her caches, cookies, and search history online? Mrs Kwela recalled the Google message alert she had received which said,*

'*Your child searched restricted topics. One of the topics was how to commit suicide, which is considered forbidden knowledge under your current parental control settings*'. *She had then opened the detailed report attached, and seen Patricia's searches about razor blades and over-dosing.*

The incident reminded Mrs Kwela of one day months ago before the sexual assault; an occasion that brought alive to her the fact that Patricia was growing so fast and changing preferences day after day…

Mrs Kwela had been making breakfast when Patricia's smart phone went off like a blast on the kitchen counter. That new incoming ringtone of hers boomed literally like a bomb! It was what the young ones called techno, trap, or was it hard rock? *When had she downloaded that?* Mrs Kwela jerked, spattering scrambled eggs onto her apron. "Patricia! What kind of ringtone is that? It's so loud!" she complained.

"It's Creative Republik's new hit single!" Patricia laughed.

"Who? I thought your fav band is Rock Nation?"

"LMAO! Mom! Rock Nation is so like yesterday!" Patricia replied and blew a large chewing gum bubble. Using her thumb, she swiped right across her phone screen and received the call, shutting out her mother. She went to the sitting room corner and talked in a low whisper. After finishing the call, Patricia left her phone on the breakfast counter and went to the washroom.

Suddenly there was a message alert ring-tone from Patricia's phone. Mrs Kwela moved the phone back from the edge of the breakfast counter, fearing it might fall off to the floor and crack the screen, adding to the so many broken screens of new phones—among them Patricia's—in the house, which were expensive to replace. Out of curiosity, she glanced at the caller ID flashing on the screen. The incoming SMS indicated it was from someone her daughter had saved simply as 'SG'. The punch of those two letters 'SG' made Mrs Kwela's chest tighten with love for her daughter. Who was this person? She used to know when Patricia made new friends, but not anymore. She had never heard of an SG. Was it a girl? A boy? A friend to Vera and Lucy, too, hopefully? Was Patricia up to some mischief? All these questions ran circles through Mrs Kwela's mind. And she didn't know the answer to a single one of them. Then the phone locked itself; since when did her daughter start password locking her phone?

Patricia came out of the washroom and picked the cereal box. She put it back down when she noticed an unread text message envelop icon on her phone, and picked it off the counter. Mrs Kwela from a side-glance saw Patricia unlock her phone using her eyes via facial recognition, and was shocked! When did maze passwords or the simple thumb press, become obsolete or so yesterday as her daughter would say, Mrs Kwela had wondered. But she did not say anything about the SMS or the SG initials, as she watched her daughter reading the text and smiling, and there was no-one in the house to ask if there had been any new school friends of Patricia's coming over. Mrs Kwela was worried, and the crow's feet at the corners of her eyes crinkled and crowded together in concern. These were the secrets that worried Mrs Kwela, for she thought that Patricia was growing up too fast. Then the rape happened, and everything had taken a turn for the worse. The sad thoughts made her grip slacken involuntarily on the steering wheel. She didn't see two warthogs darting across the road until the last minute! She tried to avoid them, by swerving the Porsche Cayenne from her left lane to the right.

Then a loud horn hooting startled Mrs Kwela. The car horn blared again, hooting ominously. Roused from her shocked stance, she lifted her foot from the accelerator. Tyres screeched behind her. Then more honking! Dear God! They were at the dangerous blind corner near the Karen turn-off, and she was almost three feet into the other lane and another car was trying to go around her!

"Mom!" shouted a shocked Patricia

Vera and Lucy's shrill, scared screams filled the car. Lulu barked short, sharp, incessant sounds.

Mrs Kwela jerked the wheel and shot a panicked glance into the rear view mirror. A big lorry from a moving firm, filled with cartons, loomed behind them…much too close! She rammed her foot down on the accelerator again. With a wrenching motion the big lorry whipped around them and overtook them! The danger was over. Luckily she hadn't lost control or landed in a ditch. But it was very narrow and up close. At least they all had their safety seatbelts on. Mrs Kwela's heart pounded at a furious rate, and she could see the murderous look the driver of the lorry, a man wearing a baseball cap front side back, kept throwing at her from his rearview mirror. Reaction washed over her, and made her hands slick and sweaty on the wheel. Her moment of in-attention might have killed her and the girls! The white-coloured lorry moved on, but not before she again caught another glimpse of the lorry drivers' furious expression, but he had the courtesy to slow down and look into his mirror, check on their position to see that they were okay before continuing on his way.

Patricia was trembling beside her mother. Lucy and Vera in the back were sweating. A shivering Lulu had gone silent and snuggled into Vera's lap, who was stroking her white, fluffy fur to calm her.

Mrs Kwela shocked that she had put all their lives at risk, sighed deeply and said, "I'm sorry girls." One needed to drive carefully in the Hardy hood in Karen. Since yesterday evening, Kenya Wildlife Service, the KWS rangers, had been searching for two lions which were seen roaming around the area after they wandered out of the perimeter fencing of the nearby Nairobi National Park, and gotten out of the natural habitat.

They drove home in silence. At their Ngong Hills Gardens, a gated community complex in the Hardy neighbourhood, Mrs Kwela dropped Vera and Lucy at their homes at the Aberdare and Amboseli complexes, and then proceeded to their residence at the Masai Mara complex. The gated community had five phases each with complexes of a combination of twenty bungalows and stand-alone mansions, named after some of Kenya's top game parks. The five complexes were named after the Masai Mara National Reserve, Aberdare National Park, Amboseli National Park, Tsavo National Park, and Shimba Hills National Reserve.

When Patricia got home with her mother, a furious, tongue-clicking Mrs Kwela, shaking from nerves of the near-accident and her daughter's misbehavior at the mall, told her, "Patricia, you're grounded! Your privileges are taken. No social media, no TV, no iPhone, no iPad, no Wi-Fi password, no Giraffe Manor, no Karen Mall, No Giraffe Center, no pocket money, no Netflix login, no swimming practice, no slumber parties or sleepovers, no game nights, no movie nights, no community centre, not even church, no nothing! You are cut off from everything. No more outings with your friends, and no visitors for a month! And I mean it. No leaving the house! Wait until your father hears about this. You are fourteen, for crying out loud! How very embarrassing!" Mrs Kwela sucked her teeth in anger and walked away.

Patricia folded her fists in anger and stamped her feet, and shouted, "Mom! One month? That's like forever!" Then she stomped up the stairs to her bedroom and banged the door shut.

The Kwela's planned outing the following day for a game drive in the nearby Nairobi National Park, which gave Nairobi the distinction of being the only city in the world with a game park, was cancelled. Mrs Kwela had been eager for the game drive, and chance to see the big five of lion, elephant, leopard, buffalo, and rhinoceros. She had seen on TV the two lions which had escaped and were roaming in the neighbourhood. The last time they saw lions was at the Masai Mara two years ago, when they took Patricia there for the August holidays, and a chance to watch the amazing, annual Wildebeest Migration— one of the Seven Wonders of the world— on the Mara River. That was one of the more fun bonding moments for the Kwela family; watching the intense, immense movement, of over two million animals migrate from the Serengeti National Park in Tanzania, to the greener pastures of the Masai Mara National Reserve in Kenya. Mrs Kwela sighed again. She would give anything to go back to how things were, before the awful and horrendous rape of her daughter.

It had been a week since the incident at the mall.

"Patricia?" Mr Kwela called out from the hallway, just outside Patricia's bedroom.

Silence. Patricia was not in her room. His deep, stern baritone voice made the housekeeper tremble.

Selina, the day housekeeper, was staring around Patricia's room, when she heard Mr Kwela calling out for his daughter. Selina's eyes were fixed on the empty, neat bed and then moved to the empty chair by the study desk. Patricia had told her she was only going out in the estate for half an hour, and would be back before her parents came home at seven, yet the day was gone and dusk already settling in. Selina heard Mr Kwela's footfalls as he went down the stairs, and she swallowed hard. If Mr Kwela called again, there would be big trouble. She made her way downstairs and to the kitchen.

"Selina," Mr Kwela started, his glare piercing through Selina.

"Yes, Sir," she replied and did a poor version of curtsying that looked comedic.

"Did Patricia go out?" He began pacing the kitchen, floor in hurried footsteps.

"What?" Selina's voice croaked.

"It's a simple question because she's nowhere to be found, and yet she's grounded and you know this! *Yaani*, you just let her go out?" Mrs Kwela, who had entered the kitchen space, interjected with anger in her voice.

"Did you allow Patricia to go out?" Mrs Kwela asked in a loud voice.

"Yes, Madam, I allowed her to," Selina said, "*Lakini Patricia alisema—*"

"It doesn't matter what she said!" Mr Kwela cut in, advancing on her, before Mrs Kwela could react, or Selina finish her sentence on what Patricia had said.

"She said it would only take a few minutes. That she was just returning a book she'd borrowed from a friend in the estate," Selina hurriedly squeezed in.

Mrs Kwela turned back to the housekeeper, "Selina, do you know if Patricia has some new friends lately? And have they visited apart from Vera and Lucy?"

Selina shook her head and replied, her voice soft and shaking, "I don't really know any new friends. Only Vera and Lucy. No one else has visited. And since she was grounded, neither Vera nor Lucy have come by when I'm around."

The front door opened at that moment, and all three in the kitchen space turned to see who it was. Patricia entered the sitting room, swaying her body from side to side to a musical tune. Selina took this chance to pick her handbag and leave, praying not to be caught in what would follow. In her heart, Selina was thinking that it was time for her employers to stop with grounding and taking away their daughter's privileges, and instead start using a heavy hand and spank her, especially after the horrible rape that happened!

Patricia was already at the foot of the stairs leading up to the bedrooms on the first floor, making as if to head up to her room, when her father called her back. She did not hear him because her noise-cancelling headphones were already too loud on maximum volume, the music almost bursting her eardrums. Her father walked to her and pulled the wireless Beatz headphones off her head. "You can't even remove your headphones to say hello to your parents?" he asked. The anger had somehow faded away.

"Hi, Dad," Patricia said wondering if her father thought she was a lip-reader; couldn't he see she had her headphones on? She walked with him back to the kitchen counter. Her mother was behind the counter getting milk from the refrigerator to prepare tea. Patricia greeted her mother, and then silently stretched her hand to her father, asking for the headphones back without looking at him or talking.

"Not just yet," Mr Kwela said, holding the headphones out of reach.

Patricia's mother came from behind the breakfast bar. "Patricia, we need to talk."

Her daughter did not look at her. Instead, she dropped her eyes and stared at her feet, as if she'd never seen the Converse sneakers she was wearing.

"Look at me, Patricia!" Mrs Kwela ordered.

Patricia turned to her mother. She blinked her large black eyes at her parents.

"Pattie, who is SG? A few months ago I saw that name on your phone. After what you've gone through lately, I now need to know your every move, and all of your friends or any new pals you make!" Mrs Kwela's voice had risen a notch higher.

"Mom, *si* you get off my back! You're always hushing my buzz! SG is just a new girl who moved to our complex, and I like vibing with her. Her name is Sheila Gundi and those are her initials. I left the house to return a novel I had exchanged with her. Will you people for heaven's sake just leave me alone? Stop hating on everything I do!" Patricia shouted.

"Hold on, little girl! Who are you calling people?" Mrs Kwela almost shouted back.

Mr Kwela intervened, "Guys, let us calm down. Pattie, you know you're grounded and shouldn't be leaving the house. But you look sad. Are you okay? Do you now want to talk about why you shoplifted the lip-gloss? Is that what's disturbing you? You've not yet opened up about that."

Patricia swallowed hard. *No, I'm not okay,* she wanted to say but instead kept silent for a good long moment then blurted out, "how can I ever be okay again, Dad? Those boys who raped me stole my okay! They made sure that I shall never be happy ever again! Do you guys know what it feels like to be raped? That's why I nicked the lip-gloss, so you people can start talking about what happened to me!" Patricia's voice was full of anguish, the pain still raw and evident in her eyes. She tried not to cry but all of a sudden, her face crumbled. She broke down and started to sob. Though Mrs Kwela said nothing for a while, her eyes glistened with worry when she saw Patricia crying. She closed in on the space separating them, and enfolded her daughter in a warm, tight hug.

Mr Kwela looked on. *I used to know you so well, my girl. I could read your thoughts, and now it's as though every day, every minute I know you less. We're turning into total strangers, and I need to stop this and make it work better for you.* Mr Kwela swallowed hard but did not give a voice to his thoughts.

Mr Kwela had also like his wife, finally come to the realization that this matter was weighty and the more their daughter was home, the more she appeared hurting and unstable. At the Karen Hospital on the day of Patricia's discharge, Mrs Kwela had been informed that a missing surgeon's blade had been found in the bathroom by a cleaner who happened to have gone into the bathroom, right after Patricia and her mother had left. Then a few days later Mr and Mrs Kwela had both received the Google alert, about Patricia searching restricted topics on their parental control settings, like how to commit suicide via over-dosing and other methods.

It was time they found a way of helping Patricia overcome her trauma and agony. Mr Kwela was planning on linking up with his wife from her Zhumba or Yoga classes tomorrow on his way from the gym, and take her out to dinner to discuss this. There was a gym in the house with treadmill, dumbbells and strap system, but once in a while they preferred working out, jogging or going on a run in the neighbourhood. Dinner at Mrs Kwela's favourite Ethiopian restaurant the Abyssinian or the Indian one Haandi, would be a great choice.

Later that night, Patricia, in her room, was mortified. She wanted to get better, and stop feeling all the angst and anger she'd been harbouring towards her parents. And ever since that horrible night of the party, she had been experiencing bouts of blackouts and memory loss which was not helpful. She got her rosary from her wardrobe and muttered a Novena and Hail Mary to assuage her anxiety... *Oh, Immaculate Mary, Virgin most Powerful, I beseech you, through that immense Power which you have received from the Eternal Father, obtain for me Purity of heart...Virgin Mary, My Mother, through that ineffable Wisdom bestowed upon you by the Incarnate Word of God, I humbly beseech you, obtain for me meekness and humility of heart ...*

The following afternoon, for a good long moment from her bedroom balcony, by the Jacaranda tree where she loved to sit, and the same tree which she'd used to climb down, and sneaked to the party that night, Patricia watched the sky. It was the last hour of the recently harsh, dazzling, yellow sun, which rose from the west every day and set in the east, over and beyond the Ngong Hills, smiling across the horizon and going about its business as usual; marching across the sky all day long, like Patricia hadn't been raped. The sight of the carefree sun was the turning point for Patricia, for it made her truly want to get better, and get her old self back.

FIVE

Halkano was deep in thought as she stared out of their classroom's windows, into the assembly ground of Chalbi Hills Primary School. The sky was dark with heavy clouds. The current heat-wave was unbearable. Halkano prayed that the rain would fall soon, as she inattentively flipped through pages of her exercise book.

As the bell marking the end of the recess break rang, and as if in answer to Halkano's wish for it to rain, a deafening crack of thunder and lightning streaked across the now almost black sky, shattering the sky in half like a pair of gigantic silver scissors. The heavens spat out their heavy beads of water in heavy torrents of rain. The students, who were outside playing, jostled to enter the classrooms. Halkano stared emptily as her classmates rushed into class.

"Halkano, why are you studying so hard? We hear you are next to be married from our village," Bonaya teased her in English so broken one could have concluded he was speaking mother tongue. The tall, lanky, and unkempt boy pushed Halkano's exercise book to the floor. Halkano stared at the class bully, wanting to respond, but the sneering and mocking the other boys made, stopped her from answering Bonaya. She blinked, trying to stop the tears from squeezing through her eyes. She stood, bent and picked her bag of books from the floor, wanting to head out of the door but Bonaya grabbed her bag, holding it in a tight grip. Halkano could no longer hold the tears back, and they trickled down her cheeks. The old bag tore as Bonaya tugged hard at it, and some of the books fell to the floor.

"Leave me alone, Bonaya!" Halkano screamed as the other boys gathered around to take part in the unfolding drama, cheering Bonaya on. The girls kept back.

"Halkano, make Sasura your soon husband-to-be happy!" Bonaya said, not letting go of the brown, Jinja cloth bag, and neither did Halkano. The resulting tug of war further tore the worn bag. Books scattered on the dusty floor much to the delight of the cheering boys.

"Leave her alone, Bonaya!" Misrat, Halkano's best friend and desk-mate, who was also the class prefect, shouted from the doorway. Misrat rushed at Bonaya and shoved him away, sending him sprawling on the floor. A miserable Halkano, thinking how fast the rumours of her intended marriage had spread in their village, knelt on the floor, gathered her books, and ran out of the classroom. Outside the classroom, she almost collided with someone who held her shoulders to steady her.

"Halkano Abaduba! What is the meaning of this? Where are you rushing to during class time?" Halkano recognised the headmaster's authoritative voice.

"Are you rushing home to fetch water from the river, or do whatever household chores you didn't finish this morning?" the headmaster Duale asked.

Halkano lifted her head to face the short, plump, and bald-headed man before her. He was not among those teachers the pupils liked, even though he was the headmaster. No pupil could ever think of saying a word of defiance in his presence. He made the rules and the pupils followed. If he found you in a mistake, he did not want to know whether you were a victim or the perpetrator. And his bloodshot eyes were enough to make you commit a mistake right in front of him if you were not in the wrong before. His presence simply made you feel guilty, even before you had done anything wrong. What should Halkano say? What started the fight? Should she tell the headmaster that Bonaya and the other boys were teasing and mocking her, because they had heard she was supposed to get married to an older man who had studied up to university, yet her parents were not even allowing her to finish primary school? What a shame!

"Halkano, you are one of our brightest students in Class Eight, but I hear from your class teacher that you have started performing badly this term, with your grades slipping. *Ahhaaa*! I see! Is it because you have started growing big breasts and large hips? *Eeehhh*? You think you are the first girl to grow breasts and hips and become a woman? I'm talking to you, Halkano!" Mr Duale shouted as he shook her hard by the shoulders, at the same time staring at the front of her dark green school pinafore uniform.

Halkano dropped her eyes in embarrassment. Anyone watching the encounter would not have been sure whether it was embarrassment from the headmaster's words, or fear of his eyes. She lifted her head and again let it fall, bitterness and intense pain filling her heart. The tears started flowing down her cheeks again. She was confused as to whom to confide in, having ruled out the headmaster, about the horrible plans that her parents were harbouring at home.

"Don't shed crocodile tears! You know it's not allowed to run along the corridor. Kneel down and raise your hands!" the headmaster ordered her. Her hands shot in the air, the way a pupil who knew an answer and wanted the teacher's attention, would have raised his or her hands. Halkano stared past him in disbelief as her knees hit the ground, thankful that the rain was down to a drizzle and had settled the dust. *Allah, please help me,* she prayed. *Why is this happening to me? Who will ever understand me, or take my side against my own parents?* Halkano wondered silently in deep pain. The headmaster lifted his cane and brought it down in a mighty lashing across her back. Halkano whimpered in agony. The tears forced themselves past her lashes and escaped from her eyes. A moment later, they were streaming down her cheeks.

Later walking home, the sun had come out and Halkano's silver, half-moon cusp nose-ring, glinted in the daylight. Then the most magnificent sight Halkano had not seen in a long while, brightened the grey clouds; hanging in the sky, a rainbow looped over the far horizon where the sky and vast savannah met and kissed, in a stunning arc of seven colours hanging in the heavens, suspended and hovering as if in amazement at its own beauty of colours in order of red, orange, yellow, green, blue, indigo, and violet. Her Baba had once told Halkano that the rainbow was Allah's art. Halkano's eyes feasted on the awesome rainbow, which seemed to arc all the way to the end of the Hurri Hills, and beyond the Chalbi Desert. She wished her life was as happy and bright as the rainbow.

A day later, Halkano decided to stay back after classes and confide in her class teacher about her father's plans.

"My father is planning to have me married off," she said.

Madam Bullo was also the deputy head-teacher. Halkano would never forget Madam Bullo's encouraging words that afternoon when she told her, "Halkano, you are very bright and I want you to succeed. My hope and prayer for you is to fulfill your dreams, achieve your ambitions and aspirations, and attain your full potential."

"I want to become a lawyer, so that I can help other young girls who have been forcefully married off, to get justice," Halkano mentioned during their conversation.

"We must fight these retrogressive cultures of FGM and forced marriages! We must take a stand against your parents. This is why the government is encouraging us to shun these ancient rites and old traditions, and use alternative rites of passage allowed in our culture, because we need girls like you to succeed. Families who want their children to succeed concentrate on studies, and put education first. I will help you. You are my brightest and most intelligent student, and remember always that the sky is the lower limit. That is the reason why you are always in the top three here at school, in all the Class Eight streams. Reach for the stars, Halkano!" Madam Bullo was one of those teachers who always had on her kindly face, a broad, gracious smile. Even when she taught her classes, ten minutes would not go by before she reminded her students that hard work paid. She never tired of jogging the pupils' minds about the fact that they were living in a part of the country different from others, and that their county needed much more progress. If a student landed in a problem, she would talk to a point that the pupil would think he or she was now out of trouble, and still the punishment would come. Now as Madam Bullo spoke to Halkano, she made her feel that there was an easy way out of her problem.

"Madam Bullo, how are you going to help me?" a curious Halkano asked.

"I have an idea," Madam Bullo said mysteriously.

A week later, Halkano discovered what Madam Bullo's idea was. After the lunch break, the upper primary Class Six, Seven and Eight pupils both girls and boys assembled outside, in the shade of the Acacia trees, and sat on hyacinth reed mats. Madam Bullo, after greeting the pupils, introduced the young lady who was seated behind her in a blue skirt-suit, "Asili Barako is the Program Manager at Safe Haven." Scattered clapping from the students assembled took over before she went on, "Having shunned the cultural rites of FGM and refused to be married off at a tender age, Asili Barako went on to university in Nairobi and upon graduation came back to Marsabit County to work at Safe Haven." The clapping became uniformed and thunderous. Safe Haven was a women and girl's shelter in Marsabit County run by a Christian international missionary NGO.

"Asili is our guest today and she will share with you her story," Madam Bullo concluded. Halkano and her friend Misrat sat close together, listening to the soft-spoken Program Manager. Many women and girls in their village looked up to Asili as a role model. Asili added to what Madam Bullo had said, that she was helping mentor those she called 'at-risk girls and women'.

As she spoke, Asili raised her right hand in a fisted punch and brought it down as if hammering the points, "My wish is the community to come together and resist the harmful culture of encouraging Alternative Dispute Resolutions." She further explained that ADR, short for Alternative Dispute Resolutions, referred to the out of court settlements amongst community members involving incidents of rape, murder, cattle-rustling, and other atrocities. After raising her fist, this time she shook it first as if gathering more energy before bringing it down with the words, "I encourage the girls to sign a pledge and vow not to let themselves be victims of bad traditional beliefs, which degrade women and girls." She taught them a new word: 'subjugated' women and girls. She also told them that the shelter was a rescue and refuge centre for girls and women who were running away from FGM, forced marriages, wife inheritance, and also fleeing from conflict. Asili also encouraged the boys to support their girls and sisters, in talking their parents out of practicing FGM and early forced child-marriages.

"Should you feel threatened, the shelter is open for you and there, your education is not only guaranteed but also catered for." This time the punch did not go down. It remained shaking next to her right ear. Asili repeated and encouraged any girl who felt threatened to go to the shelter where the doors were always open for them, and their education and safety would be guaranteed and catered for.

Halkano and Misrat her best friend and *deskie*, as they referred to desk-mates, were the first to sign the pledge and most of the other girls had followed suit and a few courageous boys. Some of the girls had crept away the moment Asili was done delivering her speech. Halkano heard one say, "My parents will beat me if they hear of this. I can't sign this pledge!" The girl then tiptoed towards her classroom. Halkano, however, had already made up her mind to concentrate on her studies.

Questions troubled Halkano's mind afterwards. *Should I discuss this with my mother? What will she say if she learns that I have signed the pledge? I hope she doesn't learn of it.* However, she knew in her heart she had already made a resolve to always put her education first and if need be, run away to Safe Haven for refuge. Sadly, a few days later things took a turn for the worse.

SIX

At Angels of Mercy, Patricia and Halkano, ever since the first day they bumped into each other in the corridor, had made it their daily evening ritual to spend a couple of hours after dinner each evening in front of the television in the communal recreation hall. Though Halkano had been at Angels for three days before Patricia arrived, she had avoided the common room and the other girls, until the two of them met. On the evening Halkano for the first time went to the common room with Patricia, and first put her eyes to that large flat-screen TV, Halkano was almost immobilized, because it was the second time she sat in front of a television to watch news and programs. That evening when she watched the television while seated beside Patricia, a look of embarrassment and amazement had etched itself on Halkano's face and she had hoped her companion did not notice.

"Why that expression?" Halkano asked, for Patricia had noticed and was looking at her with a curious look on her face.

"Nothing," Patricia replied.

"Is it because I asked how it works?" Halkano insisted.

When Patricia failed to give an answer, Halkano said, "You know the only time I have ever been near a television, was when going to the main trader's market in Marsabit town, with my mother."

The friendship between Halkano and Patricia had strengthened when Halkano ran out of clean clothes.

"Why do you do laundry almost every day?" Patricia asked, having noted that each day Halkano was washing some of her clothes.

"If I don't, then I will have nothing to wear. *Kauka nikuvae* is all I have!" Halkano replied and proceeded to wring a blouse, and hang it outside on the clothesline to dry, holding it in place with plastic pegs. Her clothes were what they referred to jokingly in Kiswahili as '*Kauka nikuvae*.' Dry quickly, I wear you. Halkano had gone on to explain to Patricia that her family was not poor, but just that her pastoralist parents believed in having just enough, and not indulging in material excesses. Patricia looked at Halkano as if seeing her for the first time, and then asked her, if it was okay for Pattie's mother when she next came to visit to bring her new clothes so she didn't have to do laundry daily, and Halkano had said she would love the extra clothes. The moment had reminded Patricia of the day at Karen Mall, before she was brought to Angels, when she had bought excess jeans she didn't need, and nicked the lip-gloss just to get at her mother.

That moment the two girls shared, had marked the beginning of a strong bond between Halkano and the Kwela family that would see Halkano and her sister Guyo, become part of the Kwela family. Pattie's mother visited once every week as was allowed. On the other hand, no one from Halkano's family had visited since she was brought there. Even though she would not wish her parents to come visit, she missed them, her siblings, and friends at the village.

Life away from home was strange and even though she was finding it more comfortable here, it was difficult for her to fit in, unlike the others. What made her not long for her parents to visit, was the reminder that they could take her back to what she had run away from. Seated there next to Patricia, she remembered how her father had called her to go meet Sasura.

"Halkano, come and greet your visitor!" her father ordered. Halkano cringed at Baba's tone. *Why was Baba overly harsh today?* She had hurriedly draped a *hijab* over her head, and moved from the shadows of the kitchen wall dividing the manyatta into two, and walked into the section which served as the sitting room. *Why was Baba calling this man her visitor?*

"My visitor, Baba?" Halkano asked timidly, the way a child asked to confirm if an instruction given was as she'd heard it. Halkano had never had any stranger, leave alone a strange man or even strange boy, visit her at their manyatta. Only Misrat, her deskie and bestie, came to visit occasionally.

"Yes, Halkano. Your visitor, Sasura," Baba repeated authoritatively, his big Adam's apple dancing inside his throat, bobbing up and down.

Halkano wondered why Mama was just seated there, saying nothing. Halkano peered at the man from beneath her lashes. *Why was Baba allowing this man to come and visit her?* Halkano wondered. She was filled with dread. *Why wasn't this Sasura guy, her brother Galgalo's visitor? He looked like he was almost forty years-old!*

Her mother stood, stretched her hand towards Halkano, nudged, and pushed her forward, "Move closer, Halkano, and greet your visitor." Halkano moved closer to the man and tensely stretched out her right hand towards him in greeting. He grabbed her hand and shook it heartily in greeting, "*Habari*, Halkano!" He spoke loudly and in exclamations. He smiled cheerlessly and temporarily, so that as soon as the smile was out, it had disappeared again.

Halkano grabbed her hand back without responding to his greeting, as if the man had a corrosive liquid on his palm and it had burnt her hand. Her father cleared his throat. "Okay, that is all for today, Halkano. You can go back to your room," her father said before he returned to converse with the man.

Halkano was trembling and felt like bursting into tears. She went back to the section of the manyatta which was reserved as the girl's sleeping quarters, sat down on her goat skin, and burst into bitter tears. She had a bad feeling about this man, Sasura.

Minutes later her Mama came in and sat beside her, "Please don't cry, Halkii. Our visitor will be your husband soon. Don't be sad." Her mama's voice was gentle and yet sad at the same time. Then she added, "my child, all I can tell you, is that our people say marriage can be like a snake that has slipped into your handbag. It can raise its head and bite you. But as women, we have to be strong and endure all that marriage brings to us."

Halkano was still shaking and didn't understand what her mother was trying to say with the metaphor and analogy in the proverb, and so she replied, "but, Mama, you've always told me that our people say it takes a village to raise a child! Is this how you are raising me? By marrying me off when I'm still a child? Mama, how could you allow this to happen? You've always taught me that in our culture, it's the wife who has authority on who enters her house. Why don't you also let me finish school, and go on to university? Is this what you meant when I got my period, and you said that Baba had been waiting for me to start menstruating? Oh, Mama! Please don't do this! That man looks so old!"

"Halkano, we can't embarrass your Baba. He's already gotten lots of money, camels, cattle, maize, goats, and donkeys for your hand in marriage from Sasura and his family," Mama said.

"Mama, please don't let that man come and take me away! You know I've always said I want to be a lawyer when I grow up. But how can I be one if I don't sit for my KCPE exams next month, and proceed to high school and then university?" Halkano sang it like a chorus, for this was always ringing in her head. Tears streamed down her cheeks.

"Don't cry, Halkii. You have to get married. You will get used to it," Mama continued. She was clearly the kind of a mother you would not get any consolation from, because she too needed to be comforted badly.

"Mama! I'm still a very young girl and want to go to school to learn, and also play with my friends who will be sad if I –"

Mama stood and walked away without waiting for Halkano to finish her sentence. Halkano's younger sister Guyo had crept into the room, sat beside Halkano, and held her shoulders.

"Please don't cry, Halkii. What's the matter?" the little girl asked, her speech bordering murmuring. Guyo couldn't understand what was going on, and so she also started crying, because she felt her elder sister's sadness.

When the man left, fear mixed with deep anxiety and sorrow engulfed Halkano. And this trepidation persisted the following morning.

The following day was a Saturday. Halkano stared for a long time into the deep but empty well. They had walked a long way from home in search of water. She wanted to die—how could her parents want to marry her off? It was not as if it was for the money, for the Abaduba's were rich, culturally speaking, with all the wealth they had in cattle, goats, camels, and herds of other domestic animals. She had heard Baba say to her mother, *I want to build a stone house and install running water and electricity, perhaps even get a television set. And stop this pastoralist and nomadic lifestyle...*

Halkano wondered if she would die if she jumped into the deep well. She stared again into the bottomless pit but she knew that because it was dry, she would not drown. The sadness had not denied her the ability to think. She would most likely end up with a broken spine, legs, and arms. Most notably she reminded herself that in the twenty-ninth line of the Nisa Surah in the Holy Quran, suicide is prohibited. To kill yourself is a great sin and *haram*. May Allah forgive her for such wayward thoughts, she reprimanded herself silently.

"Halkii! Halkii! What's the matter? You've gone all quite and serious. Please don't start crying again, sister!" Guyo's tiny insistent voice snapped Halkano out of her suicidal thoughts. Guyo pulled at Halkano's leg with her hand.

Halkano took her younger sister's hand. She was worried now about how her death would affect her small sister Guyo, who followed her everywhere like a shadow. She walked farther with little Guyo following behind. They reached the nearest water pan. With plastic jerry cans, Halkano struggled to draw water from the depleted basin. North Horr in Marsabit County was arid and a desert terrain, thus for most days the river basins and water pans dried up, and many boreholes and wells lacked water for livestock and domestic use. It was early morning and the cold and misty wind blowing along the dusty arid plains made Halkano shiver. She preferred to go looking for water early when the water basins were not full of women and girls from the village, all jostling for the little water available. Not to mention the herders with their parched throats, also looking for water to quench their livestock's thirst.

After a while of filling the jerry cans, Halkano leant on a thorny acacia tree to rest for a while. She stared for a long while into the awesome Hurri Hills, which bordered east of the remote Lake Turkana, beyond the vast Chalbi Desert, in the distant horizon. Soon she was deep in thought about her future, which looked desolate. The tears, which were always very near nowadays, trickled down her cheeks. She wiped away the mucus dripping from her nostrils with the back of her hand, and tried to hide her tears from her sister. Nine-year-old Guyo moved closer and held onto her elder sister's leg lovingly. Guyo stood by Halkano's side, gazing probingly at her.

"Why do you nowadays cry a lot, sister?"

"It is nothing, Guyo," Halkano said, but in her heart she was scared and unhappy. She was deeply worried that her sister might in future go through the exact sad scenario, of forcefully being pulled out of school by their Baba and married off.

Later, trekking back home, Halkano traversed the dusty plains while balancing a large earthen pot full of water on her head, at the same time carrying full twenty-litre jerry cans, one in each hand. Guyo walked beside her, carrying two small five-litre jerry cans in her hands. When the duo neared their homestead they met their older brother Galgalo. Guyo put her jerry cans down and skipped and skirted around the goats, donkeys, cattle, sheep, and camels Galgalo was herding. Halkano put her jerry cans to the ground too and then using both her hands shifted the pot from head to knee. She steadied it there for a couple of seconds and brought it down to the ground, all in one swift, sweeping yet graceful motion. She did this every day and with much practice, she nowadays never spilt even a drop. She straightened up and stood beside Galgalo and looked at him absorbedly. "Galgalo, can you imagine that Baba wants to marry me off?"

"What! He hasn't told me yet, Halkii, but I remember seeing that man visit yesterday and I wondered who he was, and what he was after. Only later I remembered that he works for the county government and used to attend our school. Last year he came and gave a talk at the Career Day. Don't you remember? But Sis, he's too old for you. He's in his late thirties!"

So Sasura was not a total stranger after all, but Halkano's memory could not recollect fully seeing him at the Career Day fair last year. Only that the tall, slender man's face was hazily familiar to her – maybe from that day. Galgalo remembered the talk though, and recalled the headmaster Mr Duale, saying that Sasura had gone to secondary school, then to university. Later during the talk, Sasura had confirmed what the headmaster had told the assembled students.

"I'm so sorry, sis. But how can Baba do that, when he knows you want so much to become a lawyer one day?" Galgalo had also mastered Halkano's chorus and mantra. "Has Mama tried to talk him out of it?" Galgalo asked.

Halkano tried to look away, but Galgalo had already noticed the lines drawn by tears, marking her cheeks. Her eyes misted and became watery. Halkano could not control herself and burst into tears, sobbing intensely, the heaving sobs wracking her frail body. "GG, Mama is so scared of Baba! I'm so sad. Is there such a thing as completing my education for me? Will I ever be a lawyer, Galgalo? And why can't they let me finish school and go on to university just like this man Sasura, they want to marry me off to?"

Before her brother could think of an appropriate answer to encourage his sister, they saw their father, dressed in a white *khanzu*, approaching them. He had his AK-47 assault rifle in his hand. "Galgalo! What are you doing here idling and gossiping with your sister? A Borana man is not supposed to walk swinging his empty hands like a woman. You must always carry an AK-47 just in case the rival clan come to steal our livestock. You know inter-clan raids are normal. I always tell you that stealing cattle that does not belong to you is tradition, and so raiders can come at any time! You must always be prepared to defend what is yours!"

Galgalo always wondered, if their father could ever even for a minute, desist from claiming that some people were always planning on stealing their livestock. Baba always believed in being prepared to fight cattle-rustlers and bandits. Baba said cattle-rustling was their culture.

"Carry at least a sword or a club," said Mr Abaduba who believed carrying weapons was a symbol of a man being in control of his surroundings.

"Yes, Baba. I will remember this," Galgalo responded politely.

Halkano didn't acknowledge their father. She carefully lifted the pot and put it back on her head, picked her jerrycans, and started walking away. Their father shouted, "Halkano! Halkano! Come back here, I want to talk to you!" Halkano did not stop. Guyo picked her small jerry cans and ran after her elder sister.

Halkano didn't look back but heard their father's clicking tongue, and disparaging remarks to Galgalo. "Her head has grown too big for her neck, just the way her breasts and hips have too, and that's why she must get married soon! A lawyer? *Eeehhh*? I've never heard of such nonsense my whole life!" He fixed his face into his favourite stern frown as if telling Halkano he didn't care what she thought.

"But, Baba, you can't do that. You can't just make Halkano stop going to school and marry her off to that man Sasura. After all, he finished university and is so old. Almost forty years-old! *Si* you just let Halkano, who is very intelligent, finish school and university too?" Galgalo told Baba, while moving away from him, as a cover in preparation for any eventuality like a knock on the head from the AK47.

"There's no need of girls finishing school, and university! That is for you to do for our family!" their father responded harshly, throwing a glance in his son's direction. Galgalo had taken cover on the side of one of the cows.

"No, Baba! That isn't fair. You know Halkano is far more intelligent in school matters than I am. I've repeated Class Eight twice and she's caught up with me! Please let her —"

His father cut him short. "Galgalo, you will not tell me what to do with your sister's future. I've said she's getting married and that is final! She needs to stop her *kiherehere* and *kimbelembele,* and take into consideration our people's proverb that says, the goat that arrives at the salt lick ahead of the others, finds the freshest salt, but also the hungriest python. These new things from the west, that she's running towards and embracing, are not our culture. These strange leanings are the python! Remember our people say, *mwacha mila ni mtumwa*!" The person who abandons his or her culture is a slave.

Their father's last comment had a harsh tone, as if warning that any further questioning of his decision would be dealt with. Galgalo obliged and went back to what he had been doing, as his father walked away whistling a popular Borana traditional song.

SEVEN

"Patricia, what are you thinking about?" Dr Bilal looked at Patricia patiently. "Patricia?"

Silence.

After a good long moment Dr Bilal tried again, "I realize it has been a big adjustment to get used to life here at Angels of Mercy. I can imagine that you're still scared of what you went through, and you think it might happen to you again someday, but we need to work together, the two of us, so that I can help you. What I'm asking you is to let me in. I need to know what you're thinking." The therapist had such energy he never tired of talking with his patients. Dr Bilal always tried to see beyond what his patients told him.

"*You can imagine? Imagine what?* That you can be raped and your parents don't want to talk about it? Doctor, you have no idea what it's like!" Patricia's voice rose.

"You're right, Patricia. I have no idea what it's like to be in your shoes. The psychosocial support we offer here is excellent but we need to help one another, in order to succeed with your therapy," he said gently. And as Dr Bilal sat opposite Patricia, he took on a calmness that made the one seated before him to also relax.

"I don't wanna talk about it! I just wanna forget!" Patricia said, "My parents had promised to allow me to start dating next year when I'm in form one and turn fifteen. But now after being raped I don't think I'll ever want to date anyone!"

Dr Bilal said, "One thing at a time Patricia. Let's first concentrate on your healing. We shall cross that bridge when we get to it. Self care comes first."

"So what do you want from me?" Patricia, at last, asked hesitantly.

"For starters, the nurses and counsellor say that your nightmares of suicide are still recurring," replied the head therapist.

"So you too think I'm here because I want to kill myself?" Patricia stressed her words.

Dr Bilal looked at her with an unwavering but gentle stare. "No, Patricia, I don't think that at all. You went through a terrible experience. We just want to help you come to terms with it."

"How can I come to terms with it, when my father pretends like it never happened? Like I was never raped!"

"Is that how you feel? That he's pretending the rape didn't happen?" the doctor asked.

"Yes, because he never spoke about it. He brushed me off when I tried talking to him about it. It's unspoken of at home. We never talked about it!"

The therapist flipped through several pages of Patricia's file. He silently read a full page before resuming their talk, "You mentioned during our first session that when you were raped you felt that you had disappointed everyone in your life—yourself, parents, friends, and teachers. Is this how you still feel? That you'd rather be dead? Those were your exact words," Dr Bilal said, glancing again at the open file.

"Doctor, you know when you put it that way you make it sound so simple. I just don't feel like I'm my old self. Lately I've been feeling like I'm being pulled in several different directions at once," Patricia said.

"This is good, Patricia. I mean that you know what you are feeling. But what about today, right this minute? Do you feel suicidal?" Dr Bilal asked.

"*Ummm.* Well, not really. Not like before. I feel better particularly after I met Halkano, the other girl who was married off by her father and raped by her husband. I feel I'm a little better off, because my family didn't put me in this situation unlike her."

"Good. Let's talk about that."

At the doctor's words, Patricia felt her depression was easing and flowing away, like she was in the swimming pool at school, floating on her back. But at the same time as if the depression was waiting for her to turn onto her stomach and start free-styling, for it to emerge again. And engulf her into its deep, dark suffocating folds, and drown her. Her mind went back to when she'd been discharged from Karen Hospital...

Patricia was seated on her bed. She hated herself for what had happened to her. She kept blaming herself. *Why did it have to be me? Why not Lucy who had invited those boys? I wish everything could just come to a halt.* When she was raped, Patricia cried herself to sleep every night for two weeks, and thought the world would stop, but the days rolled on by into a whole month without halting or ceasing. She angled the silver fork, full of creamy, buttery, Black Forest cake towards her mouth but when she caught her reflection on the Meru

Oak dressing table mirror, she dropped the fork with cake back onto the plate in her lap.

Patricia thought of how since her tests at the hospital had showed traces of Rohypnol in her blood stream, her parents still didn't want to talk about it. Her rape was classified as Drug-Facilitated Sexual Assault which they referred to as DFSA in short. DFSA is a sexual assault carried out on a person after the person has been incapacitated due to being injected or given a drug with sedative effects.

She had now been home a whole week after being discharged from the hospital and the nightmares were back. If it was not nightmares, then it was bouts of blackouts and memory loss. She felt dirty and anxious all the time. Her mind went back to one evening, when she was seated with her parents around the elegant Elgon Teak dining table for dinner. Her mother was shouting, telling her to stop talking about what had happened to her, if she couldn't tell them why she had disobeyed them and gone for the party. Her father's figure was still, his eyes not even blinking, nor lips twitching. It was as if he was not present. Patricia had picked up her dessert and stomped to her room with it, banging the door shut behind her. She hadn't even touched her favorite dinner of ugali, and fried sukuma wiki with grilled turmeric lamb chops with onion rings sautéed in honey and soy sauce.

Patricia booted up her iPad, and Googled what she could get about Rohypnol and other such drugs, in Kenya. Patricia liked reading sites like Kenyans.co.ke because the reporters covered stories rarely told in mainstream media. The one she clicked on to read was titled; '2 Rape Drugs Pharmacists Are Selling to Criminals.'

…Rohypnol is a prescription drug used to treat severe insomnia and assists in anesthesia, but unscrupulous pharmacists sell it over the counter to aid in criminal activities. Can cause extreme drowsiness or blackouts / often used in date rapes. In Kenya young people sometimes call it rope, bugizi, forget-me pill, date rape drug, and R-2 / Rohypnol is sold in some countries as a sleeping pill, but is illegal in others / drug is swallowed, sometimes with alcohol or other drugs. Sometimes it's crushed and snorted, dissolved and injected, or sprinkled on marijuana / bangi / pot / weed, and smoked / Has received a lot of attention because of its association with date rape / Many teen girls and women report having been raped after having rohypnol slipped into their drinks. The drug also causes "anterograde amnesia." This means it's hard to remember what happened while on the drug. Because of this, it can be hard to give important details if a young woman wants to report the rape / Rohypnol can cause a drop in blood pressure, as well as cause memory loss, drowsiness, dizziness, and an upset stomach. Though it's part of the depressant family of drugs, it causes some people to be overly excited or aggressive / Users can become physically addicted to rohypnol, so it can cause extreme withdrawal symptoms when users stop. Its effects kick in 15 to 20 minutes after consumption and last approximately four to six hours. A powerful tranquiliser, the drug leads to strong amnesia leaving victims with limited or no memory of the assault.

One investigative report said; …The Pharmacy and Poisons Board (PPB) has warned that pharmacists in Nairobi and Mombasa have been colluding with criminals by selling rape drugs.

The Drug Regulatory Authority has identified Rohypnol - a colourless and odourless pill - as one of the rape drugs that the pharmacists are selling to criminals.

The drug known in the streets as *bugizi* is mixed with a flavoured drink or alcohol and on consumption affects the central nervous system creating a drunken feeling.

Pharmacists in Nairobi and Mombasa have been accused of colluding with criminals by selling rape drugs. ... The Drug Regulatory Authority has identified *Rohypnol* - a colourless and odourless pill - as one of the rape drugs.

The victims of the hypnotic depressant experience blackouts, disorientation and memory lapse hence they may not recall events relating to the attack.

In Kenya, the prescription drug is medically used to treat insomnia or as a pre-anaesthetic but Rohypnol is illegal in some countries including the US.

3 OTHER POPULAR DRUGS

Another date-rape drug sold by the unlicensed pharmacists to the criminals is:

- **Diazepam** tablets popularly known as '*C5*'.

On prescription, diazepam is used in the treatment of anxiety and depression and makes users feel "there is no care in the world".

Criminals take advantage of the euphoric effects triggered by the drug, the PPB head of crime said.

- **Stilnox or mchele** the street name which is Kiswahili for rice, used by commercial sex workers

Like GHB, Stilnox is a prescription drug that treats sleep difficulties. In the streets, the drug often in powder form is put in drinks and renders victims unconscious. If taken in high doses while mixed with alcohol it can lead to a coma.

- **Ketamine** on the other hand, is used by criminals in matatus and nightclubs to drug their victims.

This drug is commonly used in public transport vehicles and nightclubs. Used in powder or liquid form, the drug can be injected or put in cigarettes. In liquid form, it can also be mixed in drinks.

The drug is legally sold as an anaesthetic for veterinary use (horse tranquiliser). Ketamine causes hallucinations, amnesia, high blood pressure and respiratory complications.

Patricia read another article by The Star titled; 'Rape drug' bugizi plays major role in rise of sexual crimes.

Then Patricia saw another link that sought to help teenagers. It was titled; **'HOW TO KNOW IF YOUR DRINK HAS BEEN SPIKED'**. It had ten points:

1. Loosing balance and finding it difficult to move and walk.
2. Blurry vision.
3. Feeling dizzy and light headed.
4. Feeling more drunk than you usually are and after less amounts of alcohol.
5. Lowered inhibitions.
6. Blurred speech and difficulty concentrating.
7. Feeling very disoriented and confused.
8. Feeling very paranoid and like you cannot trust anyone and being fearful of everything.
9. Hallucinating / Unconsciousness and blacking out.
10. Nausea and vomiting.

GET HELP IMMEDIATELY YOU FEEL THE FIRST TWO SYMPTIOMS!!

Patricia was shocked when she finished reading. She placed her phone on the dresser. Shortly the phone lit up twice. The first message was a text with only a smiling face emoji with red kisses and pink love signs, it was from Vera. The second from Lucy was a ghost hug GIF. Patricia smiled, and appreciated her besties for reaching out with love. Patricia switched off her iPad and took up her iPhone. She put on her headphones and got ready to listen to a Friday Podcast she liked which she'd discovered, where a teenage rape survivor, encouraged other victims on how to heal and move past their ordeals.

The following day, Patricia woke up in pain. Hot knives seemed to stab between her ears, if she so much as blinked. Sunlight peeked around the curtains in her dark room. She felt very hot and feverish. Mayonde and Stonee Jiwe's *Nairobi* blasted from her iPhone. The happy ringtone had woken Patricia from a fitful sleep. The lyrics banged around her head '...*Doing it like we do in the 254...Nai, Nai, Robi! I love my city oh yes I do! Ain't no city like my city, oh no, no, no! Nairobi tuko rada...*' Mayonde's cheery voice and Stonee raping, told the world how much they loved their city, and mentioned Nairobi's various hoods. Patricia, listening, was certainly not happy like the *Nairobi* tone, and she had even begun giving a thought to changing the cheery ringtone. Her right hand groped on her bedside table and picked up the slim, sleek gold-coloured smart phone. She squinted at the caller ID glowing on the screen. It was her best friend Lucy. *Again.* There were two missed calls from Lucy and one from her other best friend Vera. Patricia reluctantly swiped her thumb right across the screen.

"Hi, Lucy."

"Hey there, Pattie! You need to get out of the house. Wanna hang out? You've been cooped up for a week now. *Si* we go out o to the mall or something? Please say yes, and don't be a party pooper, girl!"

Patricia remained silent. Her thoughts refused to form. She heard Lucy's voice as if in the distance. The words did not make sense to her. They were just incomprehensible sounds hovering about her ear. Her tongue became heavy like a damp plank of wood, and she could not answer her friend. She shifted, propping herself to a half-sitting position. She cradled two pillows and rolled them behind her neck to hug her head. She could not stop her eyes from closing. She let the eyelids roll down and cover her eyeballs. All Patricia wanted was a deep sleep, one she would never wake up from. Her friend's phone call was nothing short of a rude interruption.

"Pattie, are you there, bestie?" Lucy's cheery voice reminded Patricia of the painful events of that dark night. Tears filled her eyes for the thousandth time that day.

"Yeah, I'm here, girl. What time is it by the way?" Patricia asked, her eyes still closed.

"Four in the afternoon. And *leo ni* Saturday, Pattie! Were you sleeping? A whole *Satoo*?" Lucy sounded incredulous.

"I'm always sleeping nowadays," Patricia snapped, for Lucy's voice began to irritate her.

"Sorry, girl, I'll let you sleep but you really need to get out. I talked to your mom earlier when you didn't return my calls, and she's like really, really, worried about you! She says you've hardly left your room this past week," Lucy clicked her tongue and added, "and that you're just binge-watching

Netflix all by yourself. Your *paroos* are worried!" When would Lucy hang up? Patricia became impatient with the prolonged phone call. She scrunched up her face into one big annoyed scowl.

"I'll be okay, Lucy. Never mind about my old folks. Come by in an hour. Maybe I'll be better and can go hang out with you and Vera. Bye!" Patricia said, just to have Lucy off her back and stop bothering her.

"*Sawa*, Pattie. My *paroos* aren't here and it's our driver's off day. I'll holla to our Uber guy. See you soon then," Lucy said.

Oh my God. Please, please make this end. Please make me be okay and back to my old healthy and fun self, Patricia silently begged in her heart. She considered switching off her phone so that her friends could not reach her, but she knew this would only add to her parent's worries. The last thing she wanted was her parents coming at her with their fretting. Tears formed in her eyes again. She let them slide down her cheeks. She wiped her nose and glanced at herself in the dressing table mirror. She was in no shape to meet any of her friends but she had to try. She had to stop feeling sorry for herself! It was as if the buckets of tears she had been crying had partly healed her. The tears seemed to wash away part of the guilt she had been carrying since that awful night.

A fresh wave of pain crashed behind Patricia's ears. Needing relief from the pain, she reached for the pill bottle on her bedside drawer and popped one of the tiny painkillers into her mouth. She drank some water from the water bottle beside the pills. Soon, she began dozing on and off.

Half an hour later Patricia sat up alert, remembering Lucy would be arriving any time now. Part of her was psyched up, because she was going to hang out at the mall with her besties, for the first time since she came back from the hospital. But another part of her wanted to cry because she knew she would never be the same again. She got so tired all the time. "*You are fatigued because you do not want to sit around others. You still fear that what had happened might become a topic of discussion.*" her mother's voice echoed in her ears. She got up and dressed, stopping to sit from time to time.

"Hey you!" Vera smiled at Patricia. Lucy standing beside Vera also flashed a bright smile at Patricia, who noticed that Vera as usual was carrying a book on innovation. Vera, just like Pattie, wanted to be an aeronautical engineer or an innovator of some sort one day.

"Hey there," Patricia responded in a flat, dull voice.

Mayonde and Stonee Jiwe's *Nairobi* blasted out from one of the shops in Karen Mall. Patricia like her besties had loved the dope lyrics when they first dropped. But now all that Patricia said to herself was, *Great. Just great.* The happy ringtone again. But Mayonde went on cheerily '*...Doing it like we do in the 254...Nai, Nai, Robi! I love my city oh yes I do! Ain't no city like my city, oh no, no, no!*'

As if we're all happy, Patricia thought. She concentrated on not looking angry, at having been almost arm-twisted by her mom to come with Lucy and Vera to the mall. *I hope my besties don't turn into a victim's pity-party support club.* Patricia knew her thoughts were unfair because her besties were only trying to be helpful, yet she felt like no one around her seemed to know just how bad she was feeling.

"Should we go grab a burger or something? Maybe catch a movie?" Lucy asked.

"*Ummm...*I don't think I feel like eating anythi –" Pattie began and then stopped when her voice wavered and caught in her throat. *Oh no! I'm going to burst into tears again. Please God no!* Patricia could not remember the last time she cried in front of her friends. But she sure felt like it right now. These thoughts suddenly brought another torrent of tears to the surface together with what she thought was surely her broken heart. How could she tell her crew, that she felt detached? Like she was not herself, and was observing all that had taken place in the third person. Like it had never happened to her but someone else?

EIGHT

"Halkano, because you've blocked from your mind part of what happened to you, I want to take over your thinking process for just a short while, so that we specialists here at Angels of Mercy can help you," Dr Bilal said, as if he could see closely what was going on in Halkano's mind just by looking deep into her eyes.

"Like you want to hypnotise me? Or something like that? I read about hypnotising in a book my English teacher once lent me," Halkano asked.

Dr Bilal laughed out loud with the same energy he used while talking. "Not hypnotise, but sort of. It's more like you opening up to me. When you came here you scarcely talked, but you have improved, thanks in part to our combined psychosocial support for you, and your hard work and determination to get better. I mean talking. Really talking!"

Dr Bilal leaned forward in his seat and stared with intent at Halkano, prompting her to respond.

"I don't know if I have improved at all, Doctor Bilal. I still have nightmares of my circumcision, and that horrible man Sasura raping me. I will never forget that!" Halkano's voice caught in her throat in a teary hiccup.

"Go on, Halkano," the therapist encouraged her.

She swallowed hard, with difficulty, past the lump of tears and said, "You know with you, I'm free to talk about my rape but back at the village it's unheard of."

"That's why we are here for you, Halkano," said the doctor.

Tears pricking the back of her eyelids, Halkano sighed heavily then continued, "Here, I can talk to you and the counsellors, but what about when I leave and go back home? I can't even imagine going back there, because my parents will just send me back to that bad man they call my husband. My Baba might even kill me!" her voice caught again and trembled at what her father might do to her.

Halkano could not forget that Dr Bilal had earlier assured her, that her parents and Sasura were apprehended by the police. Instead of showing relief at the news, sadness had taken over Halkano's face. However much Halkano appreciated the arrest of her parents, it was not something that gave her peace. She missed her village. She missed her brother and sister. The news of the arrest of her parents had not been relief at all, because they had been released shortly afterwards. But that had only been part of it. The other thing she could not stop imagining was that she had been the reason for the arrests. However, she was convinced that she had done what she had to do. Would she go back to them? If a traditional settlement of the case was initiated instead of a court proceeding, nothing was ever going to change. It would just be like a brief break, before everything resumed back to their normal practices. And this troubled Halkano. Her coming to Angels of Mercy had been largely funded by well-wishers who contributed money after her story was broadcast on television and printed on newspapers. Here she was, Dr Bilal teaching her about Post Traumatic Stress Disorder, what she now referred to as PTSD in short, and she was responding fairly well to the counselling. The problem, however, were the people back at the village. Was someone teaching them, how to not go after young girls like Halkano for marriage? Halkano understood that even after her own problem was solved, the bigger one was the village and the people's mindset.

"I understand you have become friends with Patricia Kwela. You might not have to go back to your village. I have an idea." Dr Bilal smiled. "Do you mind if Patricia joins us and you tell us the full story? You've told me some but not all your story."

Halkano readily agreed. Shortly Patricia joined them after the doctor buzzed his intercom for his assistant to get her.

Dr Bilal told Halkano, "Halkano, tell us a little bit more about how all this came to be."

Halkano had woken up very early that morning because she had not slept well, and felt a sticky liquid in her panties. She touched and looked at it. Blood! She knew it was her first period because Madam Bullo had talked to her about it, for she had been concerned, more especially about Halkano's father's plan to marry her off. And Madam Bullo had told her that getting her period meant that she could also fall pregnant if married!

No wonder last night she had been feeling sick with pains in her lower abdomen—what Madam Bullo had called cramps. Excited, Halkano pressed her legs together to stop the blood from trickling down her inner thighs and walked awkwardly to where her mother was blowing hard into the hearth fire to prepare porridge for breakfast. Her mother stood up when Halkano told her, and showed her the blood. Mama lifted the folds and hem of her *dera* dress, and went to her quarters and came back with strips she'd torn from an old *leso*.

"Here. Use this to stem the flow. I'll buy you sanitary pads after we're done with breakfast. Your father has been very anxious waiting for this day. He's going to be very excited because now you're a real woman!" Mama told her. At this last statement, Halkano had been surprised.

"Mama, what do you mean that Baba has been waiting for this day? And I'm not yet a woman, Mama!" Halkano, her voice shrill with worry, stamped her foot in frustration.

Mama clicked her tongue and said, "Don't worry, my girl. Baba will explain all this to you soon." Mama knelt on the earthen floor to continue blowing at the fire.

Later Mama had gone to the main market in Marsabit town, and bought Halkano sanitary pads. She also bought her a colourful *leso* as a present, with a Kiswahili expression printed along the hem. The expression said, '*Mwanangu amevunja ungo, furaha kwangu ilioje*', which meant, '*My child has reached puberty, filled with joy I am.*' The *leso* sometimes called *kanga*, was a brightly and bold-coloured cotton shawl, popular in East Africa, and used as a public display of personal feelings, because the phrase, expression or proverb, printed along the hem, was a communication tool which allowed people to share their feelings, without saying any words out loud. Halkano called it the talking cloth!

Their Baba never explained anything to Halkano, until a week later when a man she later came to know as Sasura, visited their homestead.

As Halkano spoke to Dr Bilal and Patricia, she did so with much ease as if the events had only taken place the previous day. And even though her lilting accent took over when she was deep into the story, her beautiful voice made her listeners glued to her vivid recollection; her audience of two shaking their heads or blinking from time to time.

"After I got my first period, I was excited because Islam permits children who have reached puberty to start fasting, I was looking forward to my first *Sawm*, that is fasting during the holy month of Ramadhan but my enthusiasm was dampened when my parents arranged for me to be initiated. They pretended it was a party we were going to attend. I remember how Mama started telling me about the party. We were repairing our manyatta using freshly dried grass, wattle sticks, and smearing fresh cow dung mixed with wet clay on the walls and floors. Mama said that the next afternoon we would go for a party in the neighbouring *boma* to celebrate the birth and naming of a baby. The following day I found it strange that we were going to a naming party late in the afternoon. It was getting dark and my shadow was long on the ground, and I knew the sun would soon disappear behind the Hurri Hills before very long. Again I'd wondered why we were going to the party so late. Soon dusk announced itself. We walked for long. Then the full moon came out, stars twinkled in the sky, and dragonflies and fireflies flitted about. I also wondered why so many women had come to our *boma* to accompany me and Mama to the party. There were many women outside our *boma* and they were singing merrily, dancing, ululating, and clapping to our traditional Borana songs. I was fascinated as usual by the stars which seemed to play hide and seek with the bright moon. One woman put a new *leso* over my head and covered me from head to toe. I remember asking, *"Mama, why are we going to this party so late, and why are these women covering me up? Where are we going?"* But Mama only sucked at her teeth and clicked her tongue, "*No questions, Halkano! Keep quiet and come with us! Just do as you are told!*" Mama whispered back urgently. The women became even louder with the singing and ululating as we walked. *Arrrrrrrirrrrriiiii! Arrrrrriiiirrrrrii! Arrrrriiiiiirrrrrrriii! Arrrrriiiiiirrrrrrriii! Arrrrriiiiiirrrrrrriii!*

We marched through the dry plains. Finally after a long trek, we reached our destination. It was somewhere in the forest. We went towards a clump of bushes. By then the *leso* covering my head had been removed. A figure approached me. It was an old, stooped woman. She seemed to have been waiting for us. I could see her face wrinkled like an overripe passion fruit, in the brightness of the moon. She looked as old as a bull elephant we had seen on a school trip to Shaba National Park in Isiolo County, not too far from our Marsabit County. I started shaking with fear, because I realized we were not going to visit any newborn baby, but that I had been tricked and taken there to be circumcised! My knees collapsed beneath me, but two women held me up. Mama looked at me as if giving me a warning and telling me not to scream. What did they want to do to me? I wanted to wail, but I couldn't muster the courage when I saw the outrageous stares of my aunts. It was as if they were wondering why one should cry, when she was about to be made a woman. I was feeling so weak but wanted to shout and scream with rage. One of my younger aunts kept whispering to me over and over again, that I was a brave girl and should always stay so. "*Halkano, Janna-i! Halkano, Jannooma-i! Jannuuma-i!*" But how could I be brave?

My dress was torn off my body, and my panties pulled down. The calabashes and earthen pots, that some of the women had been carrying, contained ice-cold water from the river, to numb me. I could never have imagined that

I would ever experience such a cold drenching. Without warning I was tossed onto a large hard surface, a cold rock, and my legs spread wide apart. I was conscious of someone else almost breaking my legs and pulling them wide apart. The threatening panic bubbled to the surface, attempting to break through the throes of fear that had numbed and paralyzed my body. I struggled and started crying while two women pinned me down, holding my hands.

I thrashed around as the group urged the old woman to be fast. I saw the old woman get out a pair of scissors and a razor blade from her draw-string pouch. I froze with fear, and wondered if she had sterilized her instruments, because at school we had been taught about HIV, and various ways the virus could be transmitted. My eyes must have been glazed with fright because I heard someone say that my eyes should be covered. A large rough palm was eager to oblige, and my world was plunged into darkness. I opened my mouth and let out a scream. A hardened hand covered my mouth securely, and muffled my screams. Mama, sensing my fear, kept telling me that it would only take a minute. One of the women put a piece of stick between my teeth so that I could stop crying, and not bite my tongue. I'll never in my life forget the struggle that followed.

"Hold her firmly!" the old woman ordered.

"Pin her down!" one woman shouted.

"Her hands! Her feet! Hold them strongly, she mustn't get away!" another one yelled.

"Pull her legs wide apart!" another added.

I struggled with my captors, kicking and biting at them. I managed to free myself, but the women were too strong and they soon subdued me again. I held my breath. My heart was pounding in my chest. I thought I was having a nightmare and that I would soon wake up but it was real. The women threw me back onto the cold initiation stone. My legs were again forced apart. I felt the elderly woman make a sudden, swift lunge at the joint of my inner thighs…

At this point Halkano dropped her eyes and hesitated, embarrassed, for she could not utter out aloud the word vagina in front of Patricia and Doctor Bilal.

Then she continued in a low voice…The old woman inserted her bony, rough and callused hands into my privates. Her hands just swiped at me. I felt sharp painful cuts. I let out a loud, wild scream that must have woken up all the sleeping forest animals and birds. The pain was excruciating. *That must be the razor*, my pained mind registered. A few sharper cuts—like someone was cutting at cloth except it was parts of my privates being chopped off—*And those must be the scissors mutilating me*, my mind registered once again, before everything went blank.

Arrrrririiiiiiriiii! Arrrrririiiiiiriiii! Arrrrririiiiiiriiii! Arrrrririiiiiiriiii! Arrrrrriiiiiiirrrrrrriiii!

The ululations renting the air jerked me back to consciousness. I became aware of a sticky wetness pooling at the joint of my legs. Someone lifted me to my feet. The sticky liquid was trickling down the inside of my thighs, and then I realized the sticky wetness was blood—mine! The old Mama scooped ash from a knot in her *leso* wrapper, and rubbed it on my wounds. The ash stung my bleeding parts. The old woman told me the ash was like an antiseptic, and would also stop the bleeding. I was in terrible pain. I tried to hold my feet apart. The women on either side of me clicked their tongues, and sucked their teeth in disapproval, and pushed my hips together, hissing at me that it was a show of weakness and that I should try to walk like the grown woman I had just become. Blood continued trickling down to my feet. The old woman was showing the others something in her palm. The women giggled happily at the pieces of flesh the old woman had shown them. They afterwards paid her and we started our journey back home.

When Halkano stopped talking, all Patricia could do was stare at her new friend in shock and say, "*Ewwww! Woisheee!* Halkano, OMG! Oh my God! That's so very horrible and cruel! I'm sorry you went through all that senseless pain." But that was only the beginning. Halkano had only started narrating her experience, and she was yet to get to the worst part of it.

NINE

"The donkeys are in the kraal in that far corner, too near the manyatta and Baba might hear us," Galgalo said to Halkano. The camels were in an enclosure closer to the gate. "Let's just take the camels no matter how much slower than the donkeys they are.' Halkano listened. Then she told Galgalo, "Thanks, GG, for helping me escape to the shelter. I don't want to get married! I signed a pledge at school, when a Program Manager from Safe Haven came to talk us that I will finish school and shun these harmful rites!" The only thing Halkano wished for was to leave home. At that time of night they had to go by camel or donkey for there were no *boda bodas* or *tuk-tuks* to hire. *Boda bodas* and *tuk-tuks* during the day usually passed through the village hooting for passengers. Galgalo and Halkano had mobile numbers of some of the *boda boda* and *tuk-tuk* drivers for emergencies, but as they had no smart phones of their own, the two couldn't risk trying to sneak into Baba and Mama's quarters to get their phones and call for transport, as they might hear them. So the camels were their only choice.

It was pitch dark and in the middle of the night. Dark clouds had taken the rare half-cusp moon hostage. Halkano glanced at the moon appearing so tiny in the sky, looking lonely, for there were no twinkling starry stars yet to accompany it. It was as if tiny moon knew it was too early to show itself, but still the small half-moon struggled to free itself, from the heavy clouds, intent on making it hard for it to show its full glory. Halkano felt like that moon; like her Baba, was intent on crushing her dreams, ambitions, and aspirations.

Galgalo nudged two camels, coercing them into a semi-sitting and kneeling position. He put the canopy for sitting, placing them securely in the middle of the backs of the camels near the humps. Galgalo and Halkano then climbed on to one camel each. Halkano perched gingerly on her camel because she was not yet healed properly from the circumcision, though it had already been over one month. They slowly rode out of the *boma* into the still night.

"Thanks for helping me, GG," Halkano said.

"You're welcome, sis. I'm just really sad that father is determined on having you married off. I can't protect you against him but at least at the shelter, you'll be guaranteed education and protection."

"I know. This is the best option for me. You saw how they tricked me about visiting a newborn baby, and I ended up being circumcised!" Halkano sighed deeply. Galgalo looked at his sad sister with a look of pity and frustration on his face, helpless and angry at himself for not being able to protect her from their parents. All Galgalo said was, "I'm really very sorry, sis. I wish I could do more to protect you! But you know how harsh Baba is! He will kill me even for just taking you to the shelter!"

They rode on in silent companionship.

"GG, are we there yet? Are we almost there?" Halkano anxiously asked after every ten or so minutes, fearing their father might wake up, realise they were gone, and follow them. From time to time, she glanced behind from where they had come. Any sounds from either side of the road or behind them, kept her alert, making her think they were being followed.

"Not yet, Halkii. But in less than half an hour we will be there," Galgalo answered.

Finally after an hour they reached their destination. Floodlights and security lights illuminated the huge Safe Haven compound. The lights at the gate revealed the tall and thin figure of Galgalo atop the camel. His shoulders drooped and if he were ever in a group of people, his appearance was more likely to attract attention than where he sat. Galgalo got off his camel and knocked on the tall black steel gate. The sleepy eyes of a security guard peeked through a peephole in the gate, and when he saw a young man with a girl, he hurriedly opened the gate.

"Come in. How may I help you?" the guard asked Galgalo.

"Thank you, Sir. My sister is in need of shelter. Take her to the person in charge. I have to rush back with the camels before our parents wake up," Galgalo told the guard.

The guard helped Halkano get her small hyacinth reed basket, packed with a small bundle of clothes and books, off her camel which had knelt down.

"Halkii, please promise to keep in touch," Galgalo pleaded with his sister.

Halkano moved closer to him and with a slight nod, said, "I promise, GG!"

Galgalo smiled at his sister as a way of encouraging her that everything would be alright, and that her safety was guaranteed there. Halkano smiled back, and impulsively reached out to hug her brother. Galgalo returned her warm embrace. For a long moment the siblings hugged tightly. Then the guard shut the gate as Galgalo led the camels away. The guard asked Halkano to follow him. She walked beside him, until they reached a building which had its outside security light illuminating the words 'Administration Block.'

"Please wait for me here," the guard said, pointing at a bench.

He disappeared to the back of the administration block. Halkano followed him with her eyes. He was heading towards a group of buildings which looked like housing units.

Shortly afterwards, the guard came back with a tall, middle-aged white woman who walked to Halkano and shook her hand in greeting. "How are you, my girl?" Before Halkano could respond, she added, "And what is your name if I may ask?"

"My name is Halkano Abaduba. My brother Galgalo escorted me here." The white woman did not show any surprise. She stared inquisitively, but her staring was more of an exercise meant to chase sleep from her eyes than probe the new girl. "My brother has gone back home lest our parents wake up, find him gone, and blame him for helping me to run away," Halkano said, guessing that the inquisitive look was demanding an answer to where the mentioned brother was.

"Come with me, Halkano, I'm the administrator. My name is Sister Hannah. It's past midnight. I'll show you to your dorm so you can get some sleep. In the morning you can tell me all about it." The tall, white lady led the way.

"Halkano, thank you for trusting us. And for sharing with us about your forced circumcision, and how your father forced you to drop out of school and wanted to get you married. I will go to the Chief of your village, and the police, and have them accompany me to your home so that I can inform your parents you are here, and want to continue with your education and not get married," Sister Hannah told Halkano.

"Thank you for helping me, Sister Hannah," Halkano responded, "My dream is to become a lawyer one day." Her only wish was to continue with, and complete her education, and defend the rights of those children whose parents manipulated and forcefully married them off, she told the Administrator and the Program Manager, Asili Barako, who had joined them for the brief meeting. Halkano did not find it easy to stop thinking that what happened to her was a normal thing in her village.

Early the following morning, outside the Administrator's office, Halima was waiting for Halkano.

"Come on, Halkano, I'll help you," Halima, an older girl, said as she walked towards the dormitories with Halkano. Halima helped Halkano to balance her brand new mattress on her head. Halima then picked up the bamboo basket which had been allocated to Halkano by the matron and had soap, toothpaste, toothbrush, sanitary pads, and other personal effects. Halkano was slow in everything she did including her speech which had a sort of weightless cadence, something that could make one assume her to be a naïve or timid girl, yet she was neither of these things.

Halima watched in amusement, as Halkano struggled to push her mattress through the tiny door, and into the dorm. She had met Halkano late the previous night, when the Administrator had brought her into the dorm. They had gone to breakfast at the dining hall together too. Halima was put in charge of showing Halkano, how procedures and everything at the shelter worked.

Minutes later, Halima watched her new friend's struggle with quiet amusement, as Halkano tried to spread her bed. Halima finally went to Halkano's aid. Halkano smiled sheepishly.

With a loud sigh, Halima slapped both her hands on Halkano's bed in an exaggerated manner and said, "Okay! Out with your story. You're too quiet and I'm dying to hear how you ended up here at Safe Haven. We all have a story that brought us here."

"Alright. I'll tell you. It's a long story. Let's sit down," Halkano said, patting the bed as an invitation for Halima to sit down.

That evening after dinner, Halkano went to evening study with her dorm mates.

Later, Halkano and the other girls took their books back to the dorm. As they passed by the bus shed, the security light illuminated a broad smile on Halkano's face. Halkano was excited there was a yellow-painted school bus at the shelter, that would be dropping her at school with the other girls every morning, and picking them up in the evenings.

Before bedtime, Halkano walked out of the dorm with Halima and their dorm mates. They went out into the communal hall and sat with the other girls, watching the small TV, and listening to the nine o'clock news; it was the first time for Halkano to sit and watch news on a TV. The only time Halkano had ever been in close proximity to a television, was at the main market in Marsabit town, while out shopping with her mother. The communal hall had long benches set next to equally long tables. However, they were so close those who sat, used the tables behind them to rest their backs. After the news, they all trooped outside to the taps to get water for their night baths, before going to bed.

"Halkano, I'm done with my homework. Afterwards you can come and borrow the English textbook you wanted earlier from me," Halima told Halkano as they walked outside, her words rolling out slowly. They joined the other girls lining up in a queue at the taps.

Suddenly, there was a lot of angry shouting, and commotion from the main gate. Halkano was petrified and terrified, when she thought she heard her father's voice calling out to her. In Halkano's mind as if in slow-motion, the constant chattering from the young girls at the taps stopped and all she heard in repeat mode was, "Halkano! Halkano! Come here, you stupid girl!" It was Baba's harsh, commanding voice!

The queue at the taps broke into three groups. Girls who had bent over basins stood straight as if called to attention. Eyes darted here and there in fear. The ones who had water buckets on their heads dropped them. All eyes turned to the gate. A group of men came running towards the taps. The men had belts of ammunition around their waists and were carrying AK47 rifles. Some the men were dressed in their traditional wraps, others in *khanzus* and *vikhoys*. There was mayhem and pandemonium. Screams and shouts. And then the terrifying sounds of gunshots when the men fired into the air. The security guard who had been at the gate was pleading for his life, for his baton was useless against assault rifles! His hands were tied with rope and the men were dragging him on the ground.

Confusion took over and caused a stampede at the taps, as the girls abandoned their basins and buckets and scampered in all directions. Basins cracked as they were stepped upon. More bumping noises as jerry cans were knocked by rushing feet, and sent metres away from the tap area. Thudding came from the girls who fell heavily, upon tripping on muddy ground, as water from the basins made rivulets. More security guards appeared from the back of the administration block, but they were outnumbered by the men who had attacked the compound. To make matters worse, the guards were as helpless as everybody else since they had only batons and *rungus*, and no weapons to match the attacker's automatic rifles.

The Administrator came out of the administration block. Using her thumb, she tapped the screen of the phone in a hurry, going to a speed-dial saved number for the police, before placing the phone on her right ear. One armed man made large strides towards her. The administrator took the phone from her ear and stared at its screen as if baffled, before trying to utter something, wishing her call could be answered immediately on the other end. The armed man grabbed the phone from her, tapped on its screen, removed the battery, and then threw both phone and battery into the bushes. The Administrator's hands were also tied, before she was made to sit on the concrete floor. The men continued shooting live bullets into the air.

Halkano on the other hand was rooted to the spot, when she recognized her father, dressed in a white vest-singlet and lower body wrapped in a *kikhoy* knotted at the waist. Two uncles and several elderly men from their village were among the armed men. The sight of her angry father, veins throbbing at the sides of his temples, brandishing his rifle, gave her such strength, that she bolted and disappeared in the direction of the dorm. Halkano's father, who had seen his eldest daughter, followed her in the direction of the dormitories. He shouted after her to stop, but his shouts added to her momentum as she ran into the dorm. She made indecisive dancing movements as she tried to locate the safest place to hide. Halkano could not fit into the wardrobe, and so she went on her knees and crawled under a bed that was furthest from the door.

Halkano had only been there for a day, and the Administrator had planned on going with the Chief and police to see her father the following afternoon. *How could Baba know where I went? Was Galgalo beaten or threatened, and told on me?* Several questions were popping up in Halkano's mind.

"Halkano! Halkano! Come out of there at once. Don't you dare defy and disobey me one more time! You're now ready for marriage!" her father yelled. He spat onto the floor in anger. The sputum shot out fast in a straight line, as if in agreement to his anger, and landed on the polished cement floor with a heavy, plop.

Halkano tried to squeeze herself into the farthest corner underneath her bed. Her father came into the dorm he'd seen her enter, looked around, and not seeing her, stood for a moment. Halkano prayed for him to go away, but then cobwebs and dust particles under the bed tickled her nose; Halkano was horrified because to her utter dismay she felt a mighty sneeze pushing its way through her nostrils. She tried to hold in her breathing, by pressing her lips tightly together, but her chest hurt with the effort. The sneeze swelled up and up, and Halkano couldn't help it as the muffled sneeze, sneaked itself nearer to her nostrils, and exploded into a loud, "*ATCHOOOOSHEEEEWWWW!*'

The sound startled her father, and he turned around and looked towards where the sneeze had come from. He saw only beds. He zeroed in to the nearest one, stooped, and went down to the floor, first on his knees then stomach, and crawled under the bed. He peered into the darkness and saw his daughter curled up in a ball.

Halkano whispered, "Baba. Please. I don't want to get married. You should be discouraging these child-marriages! I'm too young!"

Her father shouted, "Shut up! If there was any danger in early marriage, Allah would have forbidden it. Something that Allah himself did not forbid, we cannot forbid!"

At her father's words, Halkano's mind switched for a short moment to the controversial subject that Baba always brought up whenever she said she was still too young to get married. Baba would insist that the Prophet Muhammad, Peace be Upon Him, had a child bride Aisha. But what Halkano had heard is that a majority of traditional sources stated that Aisha was betrothed to Muhammad at the age of six or seven, but she stayed in her parents' home until the age of nine, when the marriage was consummated with Muhammad, then 53, in Medina.

Her father inched and moved forward on his stomach. He got a hold of her leg and pulled her from under the bed, and towards him. Finally he pulled her free from under the bed and stood up with her. Mr Abaduba's right palm made several dazzling, hard slaps to his daughter's cheeks, before he threw her onto his right shoulder. He walked out of the dorm with her head and upper body slung low over his back, her feet kicking against his chest.

"Baba! Baba! Put me down! I don't want to get married! Isn't it enough that I was circumcised against my will?" Halkano shouted, tears streaming down her cheeks. She hit her father's back and shoulders with her tiny fists. She kicked hard at his chest with her bare feet. He ignored her futile attempts to wriggle free and bounced off towards the gate. Halkano continued hitting him, tears streaming down her cheeks. All the girls had run away to hide. The Administrator was still tied up like the security guards. The Matron and Program Manager were nowhere in sight. Luckily no one had been injured or shot.

The armed men, who accompanied Halkano's father, were waiting with their camels and donkeys at the gate for Abaduba to come back.

"What a disgrace!" one of them said. He sucked his teeth in anger.

"Where did she learn to be so stubborn?" another asked, and clicked his tongue in disgust.

"Wayward child!" Halkano's elderly uncle with hair grey-white with *mvi*, spat out in anger.

Soon Halkano's father joined them, threw Halkano like a sack of maize across one camel, and tied her legs and hands with tethering rope. He jumped onto another camel and urged both camels to start moving by hitting them on the sides with his *bakora*, his AK47 rifle slung across his chest. The other men followed from behind on their camels and donkeys.

The clay and wattle-stick door crashed inwards, when Halkano's furious mother burst into the makeshift tiny room.

"Halkano! Halkano!" she shouted in anger.

"Yes, Mama," Halkano timidly answered from the corner she was huddled in.

"Are you ready?" her mother asked, fastening the *leso* wrapper around her waist.

"Not yet, Mama."

"Hurry up! You're going to your new *boma*. You know you're getting married today."

"But, Mama—I don't want to go to…"

"What did you just say?" her mother shouted, "I don't want another fight with your father who's already very, very, angry that you dared to defy him."

"But, Mama, I'm still very young and I don't want to get married. What about school?" Halkano said and stood up.

"Your father has gotten a lot of camels and goats from your husband-to-be. We need the money we shall get when we sell them to pay for your brother's secondary school education next year," her mother responded, her tone harsh.

"Mama, but I'm also just about to sit for my final KCPE exams, and also want to go to high school too, just like GG. You know I want to be a lawyer!"

"Lawyer? *Eeehhh*? Don't you dare answer me! I don't want to hear you talk back to me ever again! Hurry up and get dressed!"

"Mama, I don't want to get married. I'm only fourteen!" Halkano shouted.

"What? Didn't you just hear what I said?" her mother shouted back, her upper lip curling into an angry line. She swung her right palm upwards and brought it down in a fierce dazzling arc, slapping Halkano hard across her left cheek. The palm seemed to have accumulated all the angry energy in her five and a half foot frame. The blow felled her eldest daughter to the earthen floor where Halkano curled into herself. Halkano crawled away from her mother, and drawing her knees to her chest, started sobbing, while staring at her mother's feet which had been *henna*-decorated yesterday at the main market, for today's wedding. Her mother's feet in eye-catching styles of *yungi-yungi* the lotus flower, *maembe* the mango shape, combined with *maua na majani*, the flowers and leaves, seemed to be mocking Halkano, with their inlaid natural red *henna* outlined with the dark *piko* variety. Her mother bent down and grabbed her by her throat and brought Halkano to her feet.

"Stand up, you stupid girl. They are waiting outside, and I don't want you shaming your father again like you did by running off to that *wazungu's* shelter!"

Patricia, eyes wide with shock, mouth open wide in astonishment, was staring at Halkano. Dr Bilal silently waited for Halkano to continue. Halkano continued her narration in her sing-song voice.

"Mama, please, please don't let them take me away! I want to sit for my final exams and go to high schoo–" I pleaded but the words got stuck in a huge lump in my throat. The lump pushed itself up my throat and transformed into painful tears, which welled up in my eyes and spilled down my cheeks. The women dragged me into a circle, dressed me in a new, colourful and beautiful kaftan, and covered me from head to toe in two sets of new bold *lesos*. The Kiswahili proverbs on one *leso* said, '*Mke mpya hana dawa, dawa yake mapenzi yake*', which meant, '*A new wife wears no charms, her love is her charm*', the second *leso* said, '*Mke ndiye ufunguo wa nyumba*', which meant, '*A wife is the key of the house. She opens the house making it accessible.*' Then the women made me dance in the middle of the circle they had formed.

"Mama–" I started, but my heavy tongue got stuck to the roof of my mouth, and I started sobbing hysterically instead. The tears streamed down my cheeks with bitterness. My heart filled with anguish and fear, as I wondered why my brother was allowed to continue with schooling, while I was being forced to drop out of school.

"Be strong the way I was when I got married. We are strong women and we have to endure what is destined for us. I remember how terrified I was too. All of these women here to celebrate with you, went through the same when they got married while very young," Mama told me.

"I was shocked because I remembered my aunty who had once mentioned to me that she got married when she was still a young girl. My Aunt Kulamo had been married when she was only twelve, and had given birth a year later at thirteen. Sadly, the baby she gave birth to died barely a week later. The doctors had told her that her reproductive system was damaged. She had been unable to conceive ever since. The doctors at the county hospital had also informed her, that she had a condition called obstetric fistula, which made her pass stool without knowing. Aunt Kulamo could also not control her bladder and passed urine onto her clothes, a condition she was told was known as urinary incontinence. The foul mixture of unpleasant leakage resulted in her stinking badly. If Aunt Kulamo so much as coughed, sneezed or laughed, she urinated and sometimes defecated on herself. Obstetric fistula and urinary incontinence. Big words that she could not understand and neither could her husband, who beat her every day and termed the condition as an embarrassment. Aunty Kulamo was told by doctors that her health complications were brought on by the increased weight on her very young and tender uterus that was not yet formed properly. The stress of giving birth to her baby, and strain on her underdeveloped reproductive organs, had weakened the muscles required for bladder control. Her husband later married a second wife, and finally chased my aunty back to her parents' home. Aunt Kulamo was my mama's sister. My mother knew the suffering her sister had gone through. And I wondered why Mama was letting Baba marry me off when I was still so young."

Halkano took a short breather then continued her narration to Dr Bilal and Patricia, whose eyes were fixed on her, unwavering, listening intently to her narration of her ordeal. "At the boma I was taken to, a lot of people were in the compound filling it up. Some were seated and others were dancing around in circles to our traditional dances. The men jumped up and down wielding with their *bakoras* to the tunes of our common traditional dance songs, and performed mock fights. The women kept singing and mentioning my name. Every song they sang had my name in every line. I was getting scared and Mama didn't want me near her asking questions. My father was seated with the village elders and hardly threw his eyes in my direction. When the tall, slender man Sasura, who had come to visit us more than a month before at our home, came out of the central manyatta, everything became clear to me. This was really my wedding day! I felt cheap and abused by my parents, for marrying me off as I was only fourteen! But I was sad Pattie, because the man I was going to be left with was old, and almost thrice my age!

The women kept on singing their songs and dancing.

Later when a bull had been slaughtered and people were feasting, one of the old women came and sat beside me, and said, *"Halkano, my daughter, this is now your new home. You cannot say no to a marriage proposal, for if a young woman says no to marriage, wait until her once upright breasts start to sag and regrets fill her head! Make your husband extremely happy and you will also be very happy here. If you make him sad you will also be sad. Make your marriage work and your parents will be very proud of you, my dear."*

Pattie, my hands started trembling. My new home! My husband! My marriage!

I got more *lesos* as presents. Some proverbs on the *lesos* said, '*Mwanamke ni kama muhogo, popote aendapo unaota*', which meant, '*A woman is like a cassava plant, that grows and flourishes wherever she goes.*' One said, '*Chanda chema, huvishwa pete*', which meant, '*The favourite finger, gets a ring put on it*'. Yet another said, '*Penzi ni kama mauwa, yapaliliwapo humea vyema*', which meant, '*Love is like a garden of flowers, they bloom when tended to properly*'. Pattie my friend, I was not ready for all that!

I barely noticed the well-wishers from our village, and those from the new village come in and out of the *boma*. Finally at around midnight I realized that everyone from my village had gone and left me alone with the man Sasura. My people had all gone including my parents, brother GG and sister Guyo, aunts and uncles. GG, having been beaten by Baba because he helped me sneak and run away to Safe Haven, could not risk Baba's wrath again by offering me further help. They all left me there with the stranger called Sasura.

With sadness in my heart, I realised that Mama and the other women were right. This was my new home! I had heard of such arrangements happening to other girls, but I never thought it would happen to me. I was so scared, and it felt like I was nailed to the stool where I sat. I stared at the clay and cow dung wall opposite where I was seated. A rivulet of tears flowed down my cheeks. I could hear movements and voices from one section of the manyatta. The man, Sasura, came out with an older woman who had earlier been introduced to me as his mother, and one young girl.

"Halkano, meet my sister Darartu," the man said as he came towards me.

"You can call my mother Mama Sasura, my name. That is what everybody calls her because I'm her firstborn. You are my first wife and if you behave and treat me well, in a couple of years I will marry a second wife to be your helper."

The older woman came towards me with extended arms. "How are you, my child? We barely talked earlier." I stood up and shook her hand. I didn't respond. I wasn't fine. How could I respond? Sasura's sister advanced and also stretched her right hand towards me. I shook it but still kept silent. I recognized her face. She went to our school! A small child of around five years was tugging at her skirt. I thought that maybe the child was their youngest sibling.

The man spoke up again, "Mama, you can now go. Tonight I will sleep here with Halkano. Tomorrow I will introduce her to my other siblings. We could have done it earlier, but they were too busy eating and dancing, and they have now gone to sleep."

His mother spoke up, "Sasura, I don't think it's a good idea for Halkano to sleep here with you. Remember what we talked about? It is illegal because she's underage and you shall get into trouble. It's even worse because you work for the government, Sasura! I wish your father were alive to put a stop to this madness, and put some sense into you! In fact, Halkano needs to go back to her parents this very minu—"

"Shut up, mother!" Sasura interrupted his mother. "I'm now married. Get out!"

"But, Sasura, it's not right and Halkano needs to finish school, same as you did, and same as mysel–" his sister added, but before she could finish what she wanted to say, Sasura unhooked his AK47 rifle from a hook on the wall. "Did you hear what I just said to the both of you? I said get out!" He walked towards his mother and sister, intimidating them with the rifle. His mother and sister scrambled through the door. I was left alone with him.

He put his rifle against the wall and came towards me. He peered at the tears falling down my cheeks. "Halkano, why are you crying? You're not a girl anymore, but a grown woman and my wife. Come here!"

"I'm not your wife! I'm not yet a grown woman! Why are you doing this to me, when you yourself have finished school and university? I also want to go to university! I will go to the Chief and *Nyumba Kumi* elders and report you!" I screamed at him as I jumped from the stool.

Sasura laughed, his harsh voice punching the air. "The Chief and *Nyumba Kumi* people have no time for your tantrums! They are busy playing peace-builder with the young boys being radicalized and recruited by Al Shabaab. The Chief is also too busy settling domestic disputes, negotiating with cattle rustlers, and the fighting clans!"

He grabbed me by my shoulders and threw me down on the earthen floor. He dragged me to his bed. "Besides, I gave your father twenty camels and lots of donkeys and goats, for you to become my wife so you have to do as I say!"

I screamed and tried to fight him off. I kicked at him, slapped him, and bit him but he was too strong for me. He slapped me back and then rained hard blows on my head.

The pain dazed me and the strength left my body. He tore off my dress and panties and threw himself on top of me.

I woke the following day and sat up on the bed in shock. The inside of my thighs were wet, dripping with blood and stinking. I was in a lot of pain because I had been a virgin, and Sasura had raped me. I massaged my temples to ease the terrible headache. My body ached so badly all over and my hands were bruised. I supported myself with my left hand and tried to remember what had happened. *Where was I? What had happened to me?* I remembered trying to fight off Sasura, and the way he forcefully had sex with me, and brutally raped me. I recalled fainting. I had not eaten, and though I felt weak, I wasn't hungry. In a haze, I saw Darartu walk towards me. I had realised on my first night in the home after the wedding party when Sasura introduced us, that Darartu was my schoolmate.

Darartu had waited until her brother left for work. She placed her left arm across my shoulder, and helped me up. My feet were dragging on the ground, even though Darartu was struggling to keep me standing. We went outside. I blinked severally into the sudden blinding, and blazing sunshine, that almost half-blinded me, slicing into my brain like a knife. I squinted again at the sudden glare of scorching daylight – I'd been in the dark manyatta for several hours and it took some adjusting to get used to the bright light, and to make matters worse I had a terrible headache. Every time Darartu tried to have my feet stand firmly on the ground, it only lasted seconds before both my legs lost strength and started dragging on the ground again. After several such attempts, we reached a neighbour's manyatta. The owner had a mobile phone and he called our village Chief and told him I was in bad shape, and he needed to come with the police and rescue me and take me to hospital.

Darartu's eyes were red with anger. Some of the elderly neighbours thought her anger was misplaced. A big crowd, neighbours from other nearby *bomas* gathered outside the manyatta. Some of the people were whispering that Darartu's anger was an overreaction. *"How can a sister be angry at her own elder brother for marrying for the first time?"* one voice asked.

"How could he do this to you, Halkano? It's very shameful for such an educated man like him!" Darartu who was about to cry told me. I also wanted to burst into tears. "This means that he must also be planning to have me married off too, because I'm the same age as you, Halkano. I don't think I'm safe here either!" Darartu said, her voice fierce. Darartu's chin trembled.

Pattie, I tell you the pain I was feeling in my lower abdomen was getting worse.

"But how are you feeling, Halkano?" Darartu asked me but only a few words passed between us, for the pain worsened with the escape of each word from my lips. Darartu held my hand while we waited for the Chief and police, who had also been called by some other neighbours.

I managed to say, "I'm feeling much better, Darartu. Thanks for helping me get away from your brother. Has the Chief arrived with the police yet?" I asked. Then at that precise moment, sirens had filled the air.

"Yes. Here comes their car and ambulance! I'm so sorry, Halkano, for what my brother has done to you," Darartu said, the tears trickling down her cheeks. The police car outside the manyatta had attracted a large crowd.

"Halkano, my daughter. I'm so sorry," Mama Sasura said when she arrived, holding my other hand when she was told that the Chief and police were there to take me. Darartu had said her mother had woken up very early and gone to the market. Darartu just looked at her mother, and said nothing.

"Oh, Halkano my child! Please forgive us. I couldn't help you yesterday. My son could have shot me and said it was an accident!" Mama Sasura said.

"I'll be okay, mother," I replied shakily. They were both holding my hands. *For how long would this go on happening to young girls?* I wondered.

Mama Sasura just stared at me for a very long moment. Then told us what she was thinking...

In her staring at Halkano, Mama Sasura's mind slipped back to the conversation she had had with her son concerning the marriage, a week before Halkano was brought to her *boma*. She had tried to discourage her eldest son from marrying Halkano.

Mama Sasura had been seated on a stool a few metres away from the door of the main manyatta. An old *uteo* rested on her laps, and she cleaned the cassava that she was going to prepare for the family dinner.

"Sasura my son! You know I don't agree with you marrying that Abaduba girl, Halkano. Why such a young girl? She's only fourteen-years-old, your sister Darartu's age for heaven's sake! It's very wrong, and you know you are breaking the law because she's underage. You've heard what the government has been saying, about forcing young girls to drop out of school and then marrying them. You will end up in jail! I wish your father were alive because he would never have agreed to this. We didn't educate you to university level, only for you to turn out like this. My boy, you're such a disappointment!"

Her educated son had stood there, and pointed his index finger at her, "Mother! Don't you dare tell me what to do or how to behave! I'm a grown man! It's my right to choose the woman I want to marry, and this is the way of our forefathers!" he shouted at her, shaking with fury.

His mother didn't answer him, but instead busied herself shushing and shooing away at the chickens scrambling at her feet for pieces of cassava that fell to the ground, *"Shooosh! Shooosh!"* she hissed as she kicked out with her right foot at several hens and cockerels that were expectantly moving around her and pecking at the ground. She got up and stared into the distant grasslands with a heavy heart. The place had some of her happiest and saddest moments, but lately the sad moments had far outweighed the happy ones, like the current situation of her son insisting on marrying a young underage school girl. She wished for the thousandth time that her husband, who had died in a bandit attack by cattle rustlers, were alive. She then dragged herself, heavy with worry, and entered the main manyatta.

...Pattie, I could hardly keep my eyes open. When I woke up, I was at the county hospital and in pain. I had given my statement to the female police officer I selected, because I was told I could chose if I wanted a male or female officer. I then filled a P3 form. I also underwent tests, and a body examination for injuries resulting from the rape. Then I had a HIV test as my rapist had not used a condom. But until today I still feel anxious, dirty, vulnerable and depressed.

When Halkano finished talking, Patricia remained silent for a long while before she said, "Halkano, for me it was equally painful. All I remember was being very groggy and sluggish, and then desperately fighting off the boys who raped me. But of course I couldn't. It was as if the strength had been sucked from me." Patricia never recalled having drunk any alcohol, or smoked any *bangi* at the party. However, nobody believed her whenever she said so.

"I only drank juice, and a fruit cocktail which was non-alcoholic. But when I couldn't even raise my hands, which were very weak, to defend myself when I was being raped, I realized I must have been drugged or my drink spiked," she always said this over and over again, when asked what took place that night. Now having listened to Halkano's story, she began to realize that urban or rural, there were some issues people did not want to confront. People did not wish to speak about rape and would rather keep quiet than be dragged into a discussion about it. And whenever the discussions were initiated, they did not go beyond victim-blaming and shunning the victim of the rape. For instance, Patricia remembered a day before she was brought to Angels of Mercy, Inspector Otoyo had a difficult time getting witness statements from those who had been at the party.

Vera absentmindedly thumbed through the innovation book she was reading. As if he could read Vera's mind, Inspector Otoyo turned to her. "Vera, I hope you are prepared for your role in this hearing?"

"What role?" Vera asked with a frown.

A flicker of irritation crossed Inspector Otoyo's face. "Vera, you gave a witness statement, and now it's time for your role as a witness. You were there that night of the party, and you're Patricia's friend."

Vera's mother interrupted, "Inspector, I haven't yet talked to her about it. I wanted you to explain it to her."

Vera's mother, who was a social scientist and a widow, had been the one taking care of her daughter, ever since Vera's father died in a tragic road accident two years before. Even getting her to attend the meeting had proved difficult, as she claimed to operate on tight schedules.

Glancing down at his folders, Inspector Otoyo pursed his lips into a thin line and produced a notebook from which he read, "All the three defendants have denied the charges, and requested for a camera hearing. That is in private because they are minors." And as if to warn Patricia's parents, he continued, "I also wish to tell you that just like you have hired for Patricia a very expensive and excellent lawyer, the parents of the boys have also done likewise for their sons." He glanced at Patricia's parents.

"But why me? Y'all, this BS is now getting exhausting!" Vera finally blurted out.

Her mother warned her, "Vera! Watch your language!"

"Vera! You and Lucy have to be there for me, because I need my friends!" Patricia shot back at Vera over her mother's voice.

"Pattie," Lucy looked at Patricia, "I want to help but we didn't see them actually raping you, but only going upstairs with you. I don't know if that's going to be of much use or help."

"I just want my friends there! People I trust," Patricia replied.

"Okay, y'all. I'll do it," Vera said, her Americanized tone had tinges of despair, having realized that Patricia was not going to stop convincing her to be there, and that anything else she said changed nothing.

"Me too," Lucy finally quipped.

Relief spread all over Patricia's face. "I know my girls got my back!"

Lucy's father said, "This is going to be quite a commitment." He had interrupted his business trip with Lucy's mother to come back home and deal with the situation, because he thought their house manager was not on top of things.

"Yes quite huge. Lots of time and energy too. As you know our courts are extremely slow in these litigation matters, be it juvenile or otherwise," Inspector Otoyo reminded them.

Lucy and Vera looked at one another. They knew the Inspector and their parents were right, because even getting some students to admit they had been at the party that night was proving hard.

Back to the present and to Dr Bilal and Halkano, Patricia said between sobs, "Can you imagine that? It's the same everywhere. Unspoken of, as if we brought this pain upon ourselves. But we so badly need to talk about this!" The two girls hugged tightly and started crying.

Dr Bilal's final encouraging words to the two girls were; "From now on because you both are still vulnerable and fragile, surround yourself with friends and people who comfort and affirm you. Take care of yourselves. Self-care is very important. Do things that relax you. Take up an activity, maybe painting, jogging, hiking, learn a new sport or instrument. Learn to meditate."

TEN

Jane slowly circled the group. "Who should we start with today?" The counsellor opened the session as she walked around the small group of eight, and stood beside Susan's chair.

"Susan? Will you start for us today? We haven't heard from you in a while. Why don't you tell us where you are now?"

"What do you mean where I am at?" She frowned and then hesitated before adding, "*Si* I'm here in the room with you! But I'm still looking for my babies." Susan then tipped her head to the right side, the frown persisting.

Jane tried again gently, "Susan, what I mean is how you have been feeling lately. Your healing progress."

"*Ohhhh*! That's what you mean. I'm fine, Madam Jane. Just looking forward to finding my babies," Susan said.

"That is very good, Susan," Jane said.

The counsellor switched to another exercise. "Girls, each of you grab a marker pen and a manila sheet. What we're going to do this afternoon is draw a picture of how we see ourselves in the future."

No one moved. They all stared at Jane.

"Come on, girls!" Jane clapped her hands sharply twice.

Patricia thought it was a fun activity. She rose and went to the pink plastic bowl on the table at the head of the room, and picked a purple marker pen and a white manila sheet from the table. Halkano watched her, got up, and followed suit. She picked a blue marker pen and a yellow manila sheet. They sat down at their tables and started drawing. The other girls followed their example.

Finally after twenty minutes Halkano had drawn a picture of a lady in a pant-suit with a black robe and the small, white, fluffy, puffy like cotton wool sort of hat, pinned to her hair, with a file standing before a judge. Beneath the drawing, Halkano had written the word 'LAWYER'.

Patricia had drawn a lady engineer in blue overalls, bent over the open cockpit of an aeroplane.

"What are you thinking about, Patricia?"

Patricia lifted her head and looked at Dr Bilal and replied, "Nothing,"

"Absolutely nothing?'

"Yep! Nothing."

"So your mind is blank," the therapist prodded.

"No. Not entirely blank. I feel like I want to go home. But I'm thinking I have nothing to go back to." Tears that had been threatening to fall finally pushed past Patricia's eyelids, and trickled down her cheeks.

"You have many great things to go back to, Patricia." Dr Bilal reached behind his chair and from the middle row of shelves, pulled down a white manila sheet. A smile began to form at the corner of Patricia's lips, as she narrowed her eyes and fixed them onto her drawing of the lady in blue overalls, bent over a plane's engine.

"You have this vision to go back to," Dr Bilal said, "remember you want to be an aeronautical engineer? And you're always welcome to come back here any time, any day, just to talk to us when you feel like it."

The smile on Patricia's face broadened with Dr Bilal's utterance. That was their last session before she went home the following day.

Patricia could not believe how far she had come, since her traumatizing ordeal.

Dr Bilal had Halkano's manila sheet with the drawing of the lady-lawyer on his desk.

"Good morning, Halkano!" the doctor scrutinized Halkano closely. "You seem a little subdued today, but you're doing well, Halkano, and we're all super proud of your achievements here. All we need to do is switch your meds to different ones, because you're still battling depression."

"Yes, you're right, doctor. It's been like that this whole week too. Every night I think that sleep will make the days go faster but several hours into my sleep, I have nightmares and wake up confused and unable to see things clearly. I think the sadness brought by what happened to me is still here," Halkano replied and then with her right hand, tapped the left upper part of her chest then her right temple. When bedtime arrived, sleep refused to come over her, for every night, she was afraid to fall asleep. Every morning, she dreaded waking up. Every day, she said a special Dua for Allah to stop these nightmares, and give her peace, for many nights she woke up in the middle of the night, a crying mess, her memory muscles overwhelmed her even when she tried to suppress them, and sad, bad memories of her rape hit the back of her head.

"How does it feel lately?" Dr Bilal's voice intruded on Halkano's thought process.

"Like I'm drowning in my own thoughts. And sometimes like I'm suffocating, and yet everyone else around me in the room is breathing okay."

"But overall, how are you really feeling?"

"Definitely better."

"Good." Dr Bilal bowed his head and let out a long relieved breath. "Tell me more about it."

"I don't know why but maybe it's because I'm going to Pattie's home and not back to mine. I feel I will be safer there with Pattie and her parents."

"I'm glad, Halkano. This is incredible progress."

"But, doctor, what will happen to the other children in my village, whose parents will marry them off? The ones that Madam Asili Barako, the Program Manager from Safe Haven, taught me she refers to as subjugated and at-risk girls? The ones who suffer from all my people's outdated rites like FGM, being forced to drop out of school, and pushed into early child-marriages like I went through?" Halkano's voice was tense and agitated

Dr Bilal was thoughtful for a good long moment then he leaned forward and said,

"Halkano, you want to be a good lawyer, right?"

"Yes."

"Then you will be in a position to help them. You will get these subjugated and oppressed girls justice. Right?"

"Yes, of course. I will work hard to achieve that!"

"I want you to think of yourself as helping them in the future. Just like you have expressed in your drawing here." Dr Bilal tapped the drawing on his desk with his pen.

"I will, doctor."

Dr Bilal shifted to what he had been about to say, before Halkano had expressed her worry for the other girls. "I'm happy that you have learnt some coping skills here at Angels of Mercy. Though it will be an ongoing project as you continue healing, you will always be welcome to come back here, to talk to us when you feel the need."

Later, Halkano was surprised when Madam Christine the head nurse summoned her.

"I have a phone call for you, Halkano," she said.

"For me? Are you sure?" Halkano raised her eyebrows.

"Yes. From your mother."

For all the time she had been at Angels of Mercy, she had had no visitor except the one time her mother came. That time when Halkano's mother had come, the two did not speak for more than a quarter of an hour, because Halkano was scared and thought Mama was there to take her back home. However, her mother had spent a while with Dr Bilal.

Now a phone call? That was too good to believe.

"My daughter," her mother's voice sang into her ears. A broad smile painted itself on Halkano's face.

"Mama?" she replied.

The exchange of pleasantries between mother and daughter soon metamorphosed into an emotional session.

"How is Guyo?" Halkano asked.

"She is well and always says she wants to see you," her mother answered, her voice tensed. "And how is everything with you, Halkano?"

Halkano was really touched. But it was the news that followed which touched her most, leaving her shedding tears of joy when the conversation came to an end.

The following day, Patricia's mother visited. The two girls watching from a distance, were surprised when they saw Halkano's mother alight from Patricia's mother's car. In the meeting that ensued during the visit of the two mothers with their daughters, and the good doctor Bilal, Halkano's mother had maintained an apologetic smile throughout. Her eyes blinked in unison with Halkano's when from time to time, they locked in shared understanding of some memory. The daughter had seen in the mother's smile, her sister Guyo and brother Galgalo, and all the things and people she missed from the village, like her bestie Misrat. And in Halkano's eyes, tears had appeared but they were tears of a mixture of happiness and sadness—the joy of being offered a place away where she would be safe from her tormentors and the sorrow that she would miss her sister, brother, bestie, and the village life further.

Later on, Halkano recalled in her mind that this must have been what Doctor Bilal had meant when he that one day told her, that she might not have to go back to the village. The good doctor whose was always full of hope and enthusiasm, had taken it upon himself to strike a deal on behalf of Halkano. Having closely watched the good friendship that had developed between Halkano and Patricia, Dr Bilal had been touched, and had on his part encouraged a cordial relationship between the two mothers. According to Halkano's mother's narration to Dr. Bilal, she had really wished for Halkano to not go back to the village. If Halkano was to go back, what would happen to her was unknown, and she could not protect her daughter from her father, uncles, or anyone else. What was clear to Mrs Abaduba was that it was not going to be a good ending, and might even result in more violence.

ELEVEN

The day after the rape, police officers had gone to Karen Preparatory School. Patricia at that time was still admitted at Karen Hospital for the second day. Inspector Otoyo was among the detectives who had gone to the school. The Class Eight pupils had been summoned to school and were accompanied by their parents. The large compound boasted of neatly trimmed lush lawns that lined the impeccably kept grounds. The concrete buildings in grand architecture had beautiful bronze etchings, to indicate the class or office or library on the wall by the door.

"Y'all, this is *sooooo* like dumb!" Vera said to no one in particular. "I don't know why I'm here. It's Lucy who invited the strange boys to the party. They are the ones who raped Pattie!"

"Enough talking, young girl! We are the ones who will lead this conversation," Inspector Otoyo had reprimanded Vera, his voice stern.

Some of the boys stared at their smart phones, swiping with their thumbs fast and furiously. Some of the girls did the same too, except for Lucy; she was busy twisting her hands nervously on her lap. Then she said, "Vera! You know very well I had second thoughts and uninvited those boys and their friends, but they still gate-crashed my party!"

Before Vera could respond to Lucy, one of the boys exclaimed, "Damn! I've not heard anything about this." He was responding to a question from the principal.

"No swear words, please. Were you at the party last night or were you not there?" the principal repeated to him.

"What party?" some other girl asked.

"That's exactly the problem we have here," Patricia's father interjected, "Everyone is conveniently forgetting about last night's party, where my daughter, one of you, was raped!" Mr Kwela was alone as Mrs Kwela was at the hospital with Patricia.

"Dude, it's weird that some Class Eight girl here is accusing Forth Formers from Karen Senior School of rape!" one boy shouted at Mr Kwela.

"Young man, don't call a parent in my school 'dude.' And this is a serious matter," the principal admonished. All the students turned to look at him. The boy retorted, "But what proof does this girl have against Tony, Arthur, and Ian? Just the fact that they gave her a drink she suspects was laced with some drug? These are our hommies and buddies. Our homeboys from the estate! I don't believe they can go that far and rape someone!"

Another boy said out loud, "It's all over in the news."

"Like seriously?" several of the students asked simultaneously.

The meeting dragged on for a couple of hours with no headway.

Tony and Patrick tried to out-stare one another after their tense conversation. The two boys were at the Just Juice Parlour within the Ngong Hills Gardens, the same gated community estate where Patricia, Vera, and Lucy lived. And so did Tony and Patrick's two other close friends Ian and Arthur. The surrounding in the neighborhood was mostly perimeter walls topped with electric wire fences, and CCTV cameras hanging at the corners of homes. Jacaranda trees in purple bloom and flame trees with orange flowers lined the cobble-stoned streets within the complex.

Tony regretted confiding in Patrick whose house was in the same Tsavo complex as Tony's. Patoo, as they called Patrick, was horrified and said he was happy he had left the party early that night. It had been too much for Tony to keep to himself. His stiff posture had turned into a slump and he had closed his eyes and nodded. *Nairobi* the current hit song, which had become like a national anthem played on most FM stations and TV music shows, burst forth from the speakers in the juice parlour, Stonee Jiwe and Mayonde's happy voices telling the world how much they loved their city. Tony's ears despite his worries, like always, pricked up at the lyrics about cute girls and handsome guys who ghosted each other, '*Ma Hustler Na Madem supuu...Hii ni ya Madem waliokulenga mtaani...mkikutana Nairobi wana wave kwa mbali...I'm keeping it real...keeping it local...*'

"Tony, remember I saw you put Rope into a drink, and I thought it was your own. I didn't know you were spiking that girl's drink! And so you admit that you made a mistake? Good. Now all you need to do is to correct it, own up to your mistake and come clean," Patrick said.

"Patoo, like seriously? *Kwani* what's wrong with you these days? Come on, man!" Tony laughed nervously.

Patrick said, "Tony, *si* you think for a moment. What if it were your little sister Bella who was raped? Would you be talking this way?" Patrick's tone was full of disgust. He tilted back his head, raised his glass to his lips, and drained his Tropical Mix cocktail juice. He walked out, leaving Tony staring after him, open-mouthed in disbelief. Patrick walked back home to Tsavo complex and Tony followed shortly after.

The same day, early in the evening in the estate at the first house on the first row of Shimba Hills complex, Arthur heard the doorbell of their front door ring. He froze in his seat in his bedroom because they were not expecting any visitors, and because he'd heard the rumours in the estate. He became agitated and ran his hand across his short-trimmed, ash-blond, fluffy yet spiky hair.

Arthur's father opened the door. It was Inspector Otoyo, flanked by Tony and his parents. The inspector, as usual, had a scowl all over his face.

"Can we come in for a short while?" the Inspector asked.

Arthur's father looked at Tony inquiringly with a concerned look. He ushered the visitors into the sitting room.

"What's up, Tony?" Arthur, who had come down the stairs from his bedroom, asked his friend.

"Something's going on, Arthur," Tony answered his friend reluctantly, "that Kwela girl Patricia, who lives in Masai Mara complex here in the estate. *Huendanga chuo Karen Prep.*" She attends Karen Preparatory.

Arthur suddenly felt cold. "What about her, Tony?"

"She's telling people that we raped her at that Saturday party, at that other friends of hers, Lucy's house!" Tony said in a heated rush, anger filled his voice.

At Tony's words, Arthur's brain went numb and began to process thoughts in slow motion. He remembered having heard Tony and Ian bragging the day that followed the night of the party, about having sex at the party with some girl. Arthur was not sure if he had participated or not. The memory was fuzzy though because at that time Arthur still had a hangover, having been high on weed just like Tony and Ian were. He heard inspector Otoyo confirm to his father that indeed Patricia Kwela was accusing Ian, Tony, and him of rape.

Arthur imagined this as the moment when camera crews came out of hiding, laughing and saying it was all a prank and that they had been *naswad* just like on the *Naswa* prankster show on TV. But it was not a prank. It was reality. Arthur heard his father say to the inspector, "Officer, I think there has been a misunderstanding. I don't believe my son is capable of doing such a vile and despicable thing. Arthur is not a rapist!"

"Why don't you let him speak for himself, *bwana* deputy DPP?" Inspector Otoyo asked. He stood there, bemused, thinking it ironical, that a son of the deputy Director of Public Prosecutions was being accused of rape.

Arthur quickly crafted a defence for himself.

"Hold it! Some girl is accusing me of rape? If I had sex with someone at the party, it's because she wanted to!" he responded to the accusation the inspector had raised.

"Same here! Don't you think if I raped someone, I would know about it?" Tony found courage.

Arthur's father grabbed him by his shoulders. "Arthur! Were you drunk? Did you rape that girl or didn't you? I hope you used condoms. We don't want pregnancy on top of all the other charges!"

Arthur, breathing uneasily, stammered, "No—No, Dad! I didn't rape her. I wasn't drunk but I'd smoked a little weed..."

"Son! *Bangi!* You smoked that thing again? How dare you? Didn't I order you to stop smoking that stuff? Do you want to turn into a dope-head? A junkie! And you say you want to join your mother in the UK and attend university there? Think for a moment! Will you even get a UK visa with a rape charge hanging like a noose around your neck?" Arthur's furious father shook him hard by the shoulders. Arthur blushed a deep scarlet colour, which slowly spread across his pale face to the roots of his hair. Arthur was mixed race; what his friends referred to as pointy and sometimes half-caste. His father was black, Kenyan-African, and mother white-British.

Inspector Otoyo cleared his throat. "The story I've gathered so far is that apparently you boys gate-crashed the school year-end party, and spiked the girl's drink. She claims you then gang-raped her when she was drugged, and not in her right senses but she remembers you three. So do some of her friends."

Arthur wished his mother was around. She would have come to his defence. But his parents divorced last year.

The police officer, who seemed not to care about his dressing from his crumpled clothes, told them that they were required to report at the Karen Police Station the following morning to record their statements. And that DNA samples might be required. The inspector left to apparently also go to Patrick's and Ian's houses. Tony and his parents stayed back for a long talk with Arthur and his father. Arthur's father with lips pressed in consternation, and eyes narrowed in concentration, listened for a good long moment, to the charges that might be brought against his son.

Later, Arthur spent half the night staring out his window at the magnificent silhouette of the Ngong Hills, which took the shape of a human fist in the distance. The innocuous thoughts that these were the hills that Danish author Karen Blixen had written about in *Out of Africa*, flitted through Arthur's mind, as if he was hoping that his mother could emerge from the direction of the hills. The whole Karen suburb where they lived was named after Karen Blixen, and her home, a palatial mansion turned into the Karen Blixen Museum, was just nearby adjacent the Giraffe Center and Giraffe Manor.

Arthur missed his mother's large, comforting presence. Her blonde hair and kindly blue eyes, which had turned sad during the divorce proceedings. His parents had seemed so happy. They had met almost twenty years ago when his mother had moved to Kenya as a volunteer with the Peace Corps. For the past eight years, his mother worked at the British High Commission in Upper Hill which she referred to as BHC, as Director of the Preventing Violent Extremism programme, in the Foreign and Commonwealth Office which she called FCO.

Arthur never noticed his parents drawing apart. For it was always elitist dinner parties at the BHC, or the High Commissioner's residence in Kileleshwa just near their previous home. His mother would laugh and talk of serving at Her Majesty the Queen's pleasure. Every other weekend it was a gathering at a shindig or soiree as the mostly British expatriates called their parties. Then all hell had broken loose when his mother accused his father of neglecting her, with his busy schedule as deputy DPP. Then there was a rumour of her having an affair with the British Council country director, who was a divorcee, and also white-British like her. The British Council, which his mother said was fondly referred to as BC, was the cultural arm of the BHC and was adjacent the BHC embassy HQ in Upper Hill.

Arthur's mother had not denied the rumour when confronted by his father. Soon his mother said she wanted a divorce, and was planning on moving back to the UK with her new man. Arthur's world had fallen apart. That was when he started acting out, and became rebellious and also begun smoking weed with his friends.

After the divorce, and his mother went back to Britain, his father suggested moving houses, leave some memories behind in Kileleshwa, and have a fresh start. They then bought the Karen house in the Hardy neighbourhood.

For a long time in their home prior to the divorce, there had been no talking. No family outings. No family dinner in the evenings together as before. No nothing. Only shouting matches, which his parents had when Arthur was out. But sometimes he chanced upon them fighting. Arthur remembered his parent's last fight...

They had thought he was still out, but he'd come back early from school. He hadn't meant to eavesdrop but couldn't avoid over-hearing his father's shouted words which reached his ears...

"How could you?" his father had shouted, "I thought we agreed to always try to keep our family together! No lovers and certainly no excuses!"

Arthur heard his mother's muted voice in the background. "Don't start guilt-tripping me! It's your fault because you're never home these past few years!"

Then there was sound of breaking glass, more shouts and screams and a door had slammed shut. His mother came out of their master en-suite bedroom, her blue eyes flashing with annoyance, jaw clenched in anger, her face flushed a deep red, and thick, dark visible veins throbbing in her pale neck. Her blonde hair was wild around her face. She'd pushed past her son as if not seeing Arthur standing there.

Arthur's heart was thudding in his ribcage, like it wanted to break out. His chest had felt tight with pain. Tears had built behind his eyelids, because he hated his parents fighting. His mother went on shouting from the washroom in the hallway, and his father shouted right back. Arthur had covered his ears, and walked hurriedly away, to the swimming pool at their backyard. Their house was one of the twenty stand-alone mansions with pools in the complex…

Arthur came back from the sad memories and shook his head, trying to clear the cobwebs from his mind. His Guidance and Counselling teacher had suggested therapy lessons, but Arthur was yet to take her up on the offer. He had not even shared with his father his recurring depression. He was glad though that he and his father had found a new way to bond, through his dad teaching him driving on weekends in his Prado SUV, as in a few months, he would be turning eighteen the legal age for him to take official lessons and get his DL, and also national ID. But life was never the same without his mother around.

Arthur, to avoid dwelling on the current predicament of the rape case about to destroy his life, changed into his swimming trunks and went to the pool for his usual ten laps. His mind was on what his father said earlier, if he could ever get a UK visa with a rape charge on his record. He so badly wanted to join his mother in the UK and go to university there.

Later he played chess online with virtual opponents on his Mac tablet. He had represented his school at the national levels, and was intent on making it into the Kenya National Chess Team. He dreamt of one day becoming Grandmaster. He stared at the chess quote on copper plaque, stuck on the wall above his study desk. The quote was by Richard Reti and said, '*the essential disadvantage of the isolated Pawn, lies not in the Pawn itself, but in the square in front of the Pawn.*' This sounded like what might happen to him if he was taken to jail.

The meeting was at Tony's residence in Tsavo complex.

"We are going to fight this. You boys will all stick to your version that you didn't rape Patricia Kwela, though medical reports say upon examination the doctor concluded the girl was sexually assaulted," the lawyer who had been put on a retainer by the four boys' parents took a short breath before continuing, "The DNA tests the three of you took, are out, and they prove conclusively that you all did have sexual contact with her. The only way out is for you to stick to the fact that it was consensual."

Patrick leant forward abruptly, as if pushed forcefully, almost falling off the couch. His lips tightened. He tensed his shoulders, and straightened up, not sure he was hearing his friend's lawyer correctly. In his own understanding, what the lawyer was doing was to treat the case in a very casual manner. When the lawyer looked at him intently with an expectant expression, Patrick felt his chest tighten with trepidation. He instinctively knew they wanted something more from him.

"That's what we need from you, Patrick. Because you left the party before this so-called rape took place, you need to corroborate that Arthur, Tony, and Ian were not rowdy, and neither were they drunk, and that the Kwela girl was teasing and coming on to them before you left. And that she'd wanted one of you to be her boyfriend for some time now," the lawyer gave him his script.

Patrick leaned in closer. "What do you mean?"

"You can even mention the photograph these three have told me about, that she posted on her Instagram of her in nothing but a bikini only, and any other such-like photos you might remember," the lawyer added. "That will add weight to the fact that she made the first move. You follow each other on all social media don't you? You four boys, Patricia and her girlfriends Lucy and Vera. *Ama*?"

Ian moved to the edge of his seat. "Listen, Patoo. We need you to do us this favour as our friend, okay? That girl has lined up her two friends as witnesses. You're going to be our star witness!"

"Just tell the judge that yes you were at the party, but you don't know anything about what went down later that night. You gotta have our back on this, man!" Arthur begged Patrick.

"Hold on, guys! *Kwani* are you telling me to lie?" Patrick could not hold on to his thoughts anymore. "I saw you spiking some drinks when I came in from the backyard, where some of the students were lighting the books bonfire." And as if they needed reminding, he told them, "You were totally drunk and high on weed. Tony, you told me about forcing that girl to have sex with you. Remember your confession to me *juzi*?" His three friends were either looking anywhere but at him, or shifting in their seats. "That girl wasn't coming onto you. Ian and Arthur, I heard you bragging the following day about forcing some girl to have sex with you. Are you telling me to lie in court? What the hell?"

The lawyer leant back in his seat and watched Patrick; he had once heard him say that his three friends were spoilt brats. Arthur waved off Patrick's worries with a dismissive flick of his hand. "*Yaani*, you don't want to have our back? *Kwani,* is it a lie to say that you didn't see us rape anyone? Sounds like the truth to me!"

"What if the prosecutor asks me what I've heard you guys say about all this?" Patrick did not want to take any chances. "What if her lawyer is really tough when cross-examining me? Remember, I'll be under oath if I take the witness stand for you." Patrick could not erase the memory of Tony's confession at Just Juice the other day, and the other two Arthur and Ian, playing macho and alpha male, in their bragging the day after the rape. Even now Ian's voice rang in Patrick's ears, "*Patoo, I can still hear her begging me to stop*," Ian had blurted.

So Patrick now said, "Ian, don't you remember saying that the girl had refused but you knew she meant yes, because that's how girls are?"

"Relax, Patoo! No one will ask you anything about what we've told, or not told you. I know you want to be a lawyer but you're binge-watching too much Netflix courtroom drama series, and obsessed with a lot of American legal drama shows! We're only seventeen. No one is going to cross-examine us!" Tony tried to reassure their friend.

Patrick was unhappy that Tony ever mentioned anything to him, about what happened after he left his friends at the party that night. He regretted having the trio as his friends, because they were always rowdy and getting into trouble.

"What about when they ask you if you raped her?" Patrick countered.

"*Kwani*? I'll stick to what we've agreed. I didn't rape her but had consensual sex. Let's see who wins! That *ka*-girl is crazy! Don't worry, man, we got this!"

Patrick stared uneasily at his friends and their lawyer. The guilt was twisting in his stomach, making him sick, like he had a bad case of food poisoning. He stood up and walked out, deciding he had to talk to his mother about it.

The following morning as Ian closed the gate to their compound in Shimba Hills complex, he was surprised to find a smartly dressed man in a three-piece suit standing by their gate. From the way the man sprang into action on noticing him, Ian guessed the man had been waiting for him. Ian thought he had seen this face on television several times before. The man stretched out his right hand for Ian to shake. Ian looked across the street, hoping he'd not missed the bus. His mind was on the fact that they were still sitting their final high school exams, and he didn't want to be late or miss any papers, and get into more trouble than he already was with his Dad on the rape case.

"How are you, Ian? I'm Mr Okwona, Arthur's father," the man said, smiling.

"I'm good, sir," Ian said and shook the man's firm hand, as questions began forming in his mind as to what Arthur's father wanted with him. He now knew why the man was familiar, he was the deputy DPP!

"Has something happened to Arthur?" Ian asked, his voice uneasy.

"No. He's already gone ahead to school on the first bus."

Ian shifted his weight from one foot to the other anxiously. "Does Arthur know you're here? How can I help you, sir?" Ian's house was the furthest in the cluster of twenty in the Shimba Hills complex, for they had only recently six months ago moved here.

Arthur's father lifted both hands, palms facing outwards in a placating manner. "He told me where to find you and your house number. About this rape issue. I know yesterday you boys met with the lawyer we hired for you," Arthur's father glanced at his watch as his voice dropped to a sort of conspiratorial whisper, "I don't have a lot of time. I wanted to remind you boys that you have to stick to your story to make it sound credible. You can't afford to contradict one another." Then, as if reading from the same script the lawyer had when the boys met him, Arthur's father said, "You boys were not drunk and that girl came onto you. You did not drug anyone, and neither did you rape or force anyone to have sex. It was consensual! Is that clear?"

Ian breathed out heavily. "I know." He had not imagined that the deputy DPP could tell him that. His doubts aside, Ian was now beginning to believe that they had already won the case. With the deputy DPP on their side, conspiring and reminding him of the script, what else could anyone expect? Yesterday at Tony's none of the boys' parents had been there for the meeting, because they had all been busy, so Ian had never met Arthur's father, and was just meeting him for the first time today.

Ian walked in hurried brisk steps towards Bus Two. The long, yellow school bus was just turning down the road from Tsavo complex where Patrick and Tony lived, into their Shimba Hills complex where Ian lived. Arthur's house was the first at the head of the row.

The bus would in a few minutes draw up near Ian's gate. What Ian could not get off his mind, were the doubts he had about what had actually happened at the party. What could have horribly gone wrong that night? He did not remember anything from that night, for he had been too stoned. Did he and his friends rape Patricia as she had been alleging? He had no answer to that, and his mind was in turmoil. It was only supposed to be a simple party but now their proceeding to university, after sitting their final high school exams seemed to be in jeopardy. Especially if they got charged with rape, were convicted, and had a criminal record.

The boy's lawyer was at Patrick's house. Patrick's mother was reluctant about her son testifying, but she said that the other boys' parents were pushing her to convince him, to be a witness on their side. Patrick wanted to help his friends out, but he also did not want to get involved. Why did it feel like he was getting drawn into a mess he never created? His favourite dinner of chicken that his mother had prepared got cold because he'd lost his appetite, and was just pushing the smoky rice and chicken around on his plate. His mother to coerce him had prepared his absolute best, her favourite grilled chicken stuffed with herbs of thyme, rosemary, lemon grass, chives, coated with lemon zest and rind, then marinated overnight with a marinade of mint leaves, sweet basil, dhania, sunflower oil, and a pinch of salt. The delicious chicken was accompanied with saffron rice in coconut milk.

His mother looked at him. "Patrick, I know you're very reluctant about this, but please just think it through. Take a couple of days on this."

Patrick smiled at her. "That's fair enough." His expression softened. "I just feel that I wasn't involved in this whole mess, and I shouldn't be dragged into it. I'm about to turn eighteen and an adult. I should make my own decisions!"

His mother moved forward in her seat. A hard-edged sound replaced her polite tone, as she addressed her only child. She gripped the edge of the dining table, her shoulders hunched with tension, and said, "Patoo, you've got to help them, otherwise, I might not get those two tenders I'm chasing after. You know both Tony and Arthur's fathers sit on the laptop procurement board of the justice ministry and they decide who gets and who doesn't get supply tenders!"

"Mum, I'll think about it, okay?"

"*Sawa.* But make sure you don't go around blabbering what Tony told you about that night. The less you say, the better off you all are going to be. Tony seems concerned that you think they want you to lie. I assure you that no one wants you to lie. Just stick to the fact that the boys were not drunk and that girl was teasing and coming on to them," his mother said in finality. The lawyer was intently watching the exchange between mother and son.

"Okay, I get it!" Patrick snapped. "And you know I don't blabber!"

"Good. I just want to make absolutely sure and certain, that you understand why this is so crucial. The private university you want to attend to study law doesn't come cheap. And me being a single mother, I have to make sure as a businesswoman I get these tenders which will pay for that very expensive tuition!"

"I understand, Mum."

"Good for you, son!"

The boys' lawyer, who had come by to talk to Patrick and his mother, and had spent the past couple of minutes watching their back and forth conversation, stood to leave. He walked towards the main door and turned the knob.

"Excuse me, sir," Patrick stopped him, "You guys keep saying I'm one of three that Tony told this about. Who are the other two? I know it can't be Arthur and Ian, because they were there with Tony on that night."

"Your mother is right, Patrick," the lawyer replied as if he was only making a comment and not answering any question. "The less you know, the better. The less you talk, the better." The lawyer smiled his characteristic, enigmatic, curling of the corner of his lips, accompanied with a slight lifting of the brows and walked out.

Ian was seated with his aunt and uncle who were visiting, but he looked straight ahead, avoiding their eyes. "I have to pass my finals because I'm in enough trouble as it is, Aunt."

"Oh, really? Is this what your mother referred to over the phone about you being in a kind of tough situation? What have you been up to this time, dear? Is it a teenage thing? A phase?" his aunt probed. Ian's mother was away for a whole year in Germany pursuing her Doctoral studies on a scholarship, and so occasionally his aunts and uncles passed by to check up on him and his Dad. Ian had no siblings. He nervously shifted in his chair. So his mum had already called her sister and brother to tell them about it?

"My dear sis, you know phases become habits, and habits become problems!" his uncle said, looking at his sister.

"*Si* we got a little carried away last week at a party, and some girl is now accusing us of rape," Ian said, his voice hesitant.

"Mmmm. Rape is a horrible thing and you say you got a little carried away, Ian? I hope you used condoms at the very least!" His uncle let out a hard, harsh mirthless laughter.

"*Awwww*, come on, Uncle! We didn't do it."

"Who is 'we'?" his aunt asked.

"Tony, Arthur, and myself," Ian replied, his voice still low.

"I heard about this, and a little bird told me you might be put on probation. If that happens you should count yourself lucky that you don't end up in jail. We've brought you up well and stressed to you how important it is to respect women, but I just don't know what's happening to you lately. In a few months you're soon turning eighteen, and will be an adult!" his uncle added.

"By the way, Uncle," Ian started, his voice a bit shaky, "Will you be very busy tomorrow afternoon? I was wondering if you would have time for us to talk about this—"

Ian's father walked into the room at that moment. Ian pretended he was flipping through a magazine, because he felt he'd had enough fights with his father on the rape case to last a lifetime. His father had been insisting that Ian should carry his own cross.

Patrick was tidying up his locker. He and his classmates were clearing out their personal belongings, for they were just about to sit their final exam paper, be done with high school, and hand over the locker keys to the head prefect. Patrick's mood was not made any better, for his mind was preoccupied with trying to avoid certain people. He was almost oblivious to the excitement surrounding him, of the other students rushing back and forth in the corridor. He was glad though that he had managed to avoid Ian, Arthur, Tony, and their parents for a couple of days. He glanced at his phone. Their calls and text messages were exasperating.

Text me when you're done with your paper. SMS from Ian.

You aren't done yet? One-line Gmail from Arthur.

????? Text from Tony. Just question marks, as if Patrick like a detective should decipher their meaning.

WTH??? Can you please get in touch? A text from Tony.
Several voicemails from some of their parents.
More than twenty missed calls from all of them.
NKT!! From Ian.
Red-faced angry emojis from his friends.
More wide-eyed exasperated emojis from them.

Patrick ignored the beeps and bleeps. He removed his wireless headphones, and put his phone on silent mode. He muted all Instagram, Snapchat, and social media apps and pushed the phone into the back of the locker. *Serves them right!*

He headed to the library. That afternoon's Chemistry paper would be a tough one. He hoped his friends were not at the library.

"How did it come up, Tony?" his mother asked him, "How on earth did you end up being so indiscreet to Patrick?" His mother levelled her steady gaze at him.

"*Si* I just mentioned that we were at the party and I hooked up with this girl," Tony replied, hanging his head in embarrassment.

"How long after the party? After how many days did you tell him about it?" his mother persisted. "You know in these sorts of investigations, timelines matter a lot."

"I don't remember precisely," Tony said, his voice low.

"Son, you don't remember anything nowadays!" his mother reprimanded.

Both Tony's parents stood and began pacing around the sitting room, deep in thought. His mother stopped tersely as if rooted to the spot, "Tony, I heard from Okwona, Arthur's father that the CCTV footage obtained from Lucy's house shows you three boys going upstairs with Patricia! And that the rape kit has been processed, and there's conclusive evidence of your DNA all over it, after the tests you three boys took! Arthur's father is deputy DPP. You know, deputy to the Director of Public Prosecutions, so Okwona knows what he's talking about. We need to get rid of that evidence, or make sure that Patrick shuts his mouth, so that the prosecution will have nothing!"

His father returned to his seat and flopped down like he was exhausted, his knees on elbows, palms on cheeks and said his tone exasperated, "Tony, can you please try to remember what you told Patrick about that night? You know if he refuses to be a witness for you guys as the defendants, and instead turns up for the prosecution, you'll have to remember what you told him, and counter whatever he says. That is if you are being truthful and didn't rape that girl, son!"

"Dad, I told him nothing! Just that I hooked up with a girl."

"Did you mention the girl's name, or tell him that you had sex with her?" his mother pounced, giving no prior warning.

"No, Mum. He didn't ask. But I'm also not too sure of what I said, and didn't say anymore!" Tony shouted.

His father shot up again and started pacing, joining his mother who had also resumed her back and forth across the sitting room. Their son's outburst stopped both of them in their tracks. They both turned as if on cue, and stared at him. His father spoke first, "Tony, hold on there for a minute, son! You're not sure anymore of what you told him?"

"Yeah," Tony coughed, "I'm just not so—so sure anymore." His voice wavered.

They both looked at him, stunned. His mother sighed in exasperation. "You stupid boy! You just couldn't keep it to yourself, could you? You felt dope confessing! Is that what you call it? Dope!" Her voice harsh, she looked like she could strangle her son with her bare hands. "Your reputation and ours as a family is at stake here. This is all over the news! Can you imagine what example you're setting for your younger sister? She's only ten! You might go to jail and not university, you fool! Can you imagine having a criminal record for the rest of your life?" Tony cringed at his mother's harsh tone. Their university lecturer mother had always been the strict one and disciplinarian in the family, more than their architect father.

"We need to get rid of that DNA kit," his mother said again. "The rape kit also showed the girl had traces of Rophynol in her bloodstream, I hear you kids call it bugizi or rope! It's a damn shame, you know? Being accused of a DFSA crime! Imagine Drug-facilitated sexual assault! We have to get rid of that rape kit!"

"No!" his father countered. "Tony needs to face the music and that means owning up to his mistakes! Tony, we've brought you up well and we're not going to start covering up for your foolishness and mistakes. I completely disagree with your mother on this one."

"But, Dad, I can't go to jail—" Tony pleaded.

"I've said no! You take this like the man I've taught you to be. You're turning eighteen in only a few months' time, and that's adult! And I hope you used condoms! Can you just for a moment imagine if it was your sister who'd been raped? If you're guilty of rape and sent to jail, so be it! And that's final! Choices have consequences!" his father said.

Tony, feeling ashamed, dropped his eyes. He was for sure grateful that his little sister Bella, the only sibling he had, was away at a Brownie Cadet's boot camp, and not at home to witness all the drama!

TWELVE

Patricia was on the phone with her mother. She was using the wireless phone in her room, which was programmed to only allow calls to her house number. Her parents had insisted she leave her iPhone and iPad at home, and concentrate on her healing when she was booked at Angels.

"Mom? Will you be coming with Daddy to pick me up tomorrow?"

"Hi, baby! Of course your father will come with me."

Though Patricia knew her mother could not see her, she smiled into the phone.

"Mom, I hope you haven't changed your mind about Halkano coming to live with us. She really needs to get away from her father, and her mother has allowed her to come live with us. You said so last week after your discussion with her mother and Doctor Bilal."

"Honey—" Mrs Kwela called out to Patricia's father. "It's Pattie. Please remember we're picking her and Halkano tomorrow."

Mr Kwela went over and took the phone from his wife. "Pattie? Of course we can't forget, my dear. We shall be there on time tomorrow."

Patricia felt that her father, just like in the recent past when they had talked, sounded preoccupied. She took a deep breath before answering her father, "*Sawa,* Dad. See you *kesho,*" and hung up.

A little while later, Jane opened the door and entered the group therapy room holding a young girl's hand. "Girls, meet Brenda. She's joining us today for the first time."

"Hi, Brenda," several voices chorused.

Jane led Brenda to an empty chair. "Brenda, why don't you tell us something about yourself."

Brenda suddenly let out a loud wild scream. "Get those boys away from me! They raped me! They raped me!"

Halkano and Patricia looked at each other sadly when they heard the word rape coming from another young girl, who looked even younger than them. The new girl stood from the chair, turned around, and ran to the corner of the room where she huddled in the corner and screamed again that the boys were going to rape her. Her high-pitched voice drew the attention of the nurse on standby, in the nurse's station opposite the group therapy room. The nurse came into the room with a lady orderly who helped her take Brenda away to calm her down.

A sad, uncomfortable silence took over and lasted a couple of minutes before Jane spoke. "Girls, Halkano and Patricia have something to tell the group," she announced.

Patricia and Halkano both stood at the same time. Patricia took a deep breath and exhaled slowly. "We're leaving tomorrow."

Halkano added, "We didn't want to leave without saying goodbye, because you girls have been like family to us these past few weeks."

The other girls looked on in silence. Susan finally took the lead and spoke up, "Thank you for letting us know. At least you won't just disappear like my twins!" They all burst out laughing, stood up and shared a group hug.

The following day after lunch, Patricia waited patiently for her mother to answer her phone. When her mother did not return the missed calls, Patricia went to the common room to look for Halkano, who earlier was also already packed and ready to leave. Susan told Patricia that Halkano had gone back to her room, to get something she had forgotten.

The common room was noisy. Patricia pulled her sweatshirt's hood over her ears. "OMG, sooooo loud!" she said to no one in particular. "Why are you people always sooooo loud?" When no one answered her, she decided to take a walk in the garden. She was outside admiring the beautiful well-tended hibiscus and bougainvillea flowers by the jacaranda tree also in full purple bloom, when a familiar voice called out to her.

"Hello, Patricia?"

She turned and her eyes confirmed the familiar voice. Her mind quickly reminded her that this could be an opportunity.

"Could you please help me with your phone? I would like to text my mother."

Jane agreed and handed her the phone.

Patricia moved a few steps away to a secluded corner of the garden. She texted fast, thumbs fleeting hurriedly over the keypad, *'Mom, where are you? I called you from the wireless but you haven't returned my calls! Did you forget to pick us up??!! This is Jane, the counselor's phone. I've just borrowed it to text you.'* For good measure she added two angry red-faced emojis at the end of her SMS.

A minute later her mother texted back, *'Sorry, dear. I was held up in a meeting that overlapped with another. I'll be there in 20.'* Her mother added a smiling emoji which looked apologetic with a scrunched up face and hands over the head.

'K'. Patricia texted back. She handed the phone back to Jane and thanked her. Patricia went back to her room.

Later the knock Patricia had been waiting for on the door of her room finally came.

"Patricia, it's time to go!" Patricia recognized Christine, the head nurse's voice. "Your parents are here. I'll go get Halkano."

Patricia scrambled out of bed and jumped to the floor. She rushed off to get her stuff that had been inventoried, when she arrived at Angel's on that first day almost two months ago.

Once home, Patricia's father removed his blazer, paced up and down the sitting room, and finally said, "Pattie baby, I'm really sorry that I've been aloof. I guess it was the shock of dealing with the fact that my baby had been raped." He went over and knelt at Patricia's feet where she was seated. "From what Dr Bilal told us, I think it's my fault that you've been feeling you can't speak to us about what happened to you. I'm so very sorry. Please forgive me."

Mr Kwela got up, sat beside his daughter on the couch, pulled her up to him, and hugged her. Halkano, seated on the extreme side of the couch, stared at Patricia being hugged by her father. A shadow of pain fleeted across her face, for Halkano missed her Mama's embrace and customary cheek to cheek kisses they always exchanged. The last time her Mama had hugged her was when she came to Angels, and it was as if it was a way of saying a final goodbye. That visit was etched in Halkano's memory.

Before Patricia's father released her, he whispered to her, "We'll get through this together."

Patricia looked at her mother who was seated on the next couch and told her, "Mom, please forgive me. You too, Daddy. I now agree and do take some responsibility, that I should have called you on the night of the party when it got rowdy."

Patricia's parents both got up and pulled her to her feet. "No, Pattie. We're the ones who are sorry for trying to pretend the rape didn't happen." Patricia's mother stretched out her hand and pulled Halkano into the tiny circle they had made. All four of them hugged. "We shall all get through this together. We promise. Soon you two will be back to your sassy, outgoing, happy, and energetic old selves!" Mrs Kwela said.

"Mom, you're right. We shall be fine. The therapist told us that ultimately to be fine is our choice. We were taught to forget the 'Why', as in asking 'Why did this happen to us', and instead concentrate on the 'How', as in 'How do we heal' and put this behind us. That way we can avoid bad vibes and focus on the good," Patricia added.

"Yes, Mrs Kwela," quipped Halkano. "We focus on our blessings and positive energy from now on! We look out for the okay and the good in our lives, and not dwell too much on the negative. We were also told that we should not blame ourselves so much, and that the offenders, too, and the society need to change and accept us."

"Good," Mr Kwela said, "Pattie, why don't you show Halkano around the house and then the guest room. That will be her bedroom from now on. The tutor we have hired to get her ready for school, will be here in two hours for a short orientation."

Halkano's eyes swept across the guest bedroom. She was shocked. This was her room? She had never seen anything like it in her whole life. The room was huge and decorated in purple and maroon. But Pattie said it was not purple and maroon, but lilac and fuchsia. Halkano's feet sank into the soft plush carpet with an orange-ish shade, which again Pattie corrected her and called magenta. The bed in the middle of the room was so huge that Halkano's slim frame appeared lost in the soft, warm layers, of duvets and comforters. There was even a bathroom in the bedroom, so she did not have to go out to the one in the hallway.

"I'm still semi-grounded about going out unaccompanied, and my parents took away my privileges because I went to that party without their permission," Patricia told Halkano who was in deep admiration of the room and was not even listening. "My grounding punishment also has to do with something wrong I did at the mall, which I'll tell you about one day. My privileges being taken away, means that I have no phone and computer for one more week, and many other things. But it's better than being completely grounded, that is not going out at all!" Patricia continued.

"So, what will you do?" Halkano asked

"Don't worry about that, but you must have social media accounts ASAP! Next week I will show you how to open up a Facebook account, a Snapchat, Instagram, and TikTok accounts."

"*Sawa*," Halkano eagerly agreed.

"By the way, we say IG instead of Instagram in full. The internet is very exciting, though of course my parents have blocked access to some sites, which can be very dangerous and lure young people into doing bad things." Patricia fit in perfectly into her role of giving Halkano orientation. "My parents said that they will get you a computer tutor next week because at your new school, you will use computers all the time and do some of your assignments here at home and email them to your teachers. See that computer on the desk beside the dressing table? That is yours. I can show you how to switch it on and off and how to do a few things," Patricia explained to Halkano. Halkano had nothing just yet to say. She had a lot to get used to. Her eyes roamed around the room.

In her heart, Halkano wondered if the computer was really all her own. She stared at the shiny chrome laptop open on the study table, in complete disbelief. Beside the laptop was what Pattie said was a PlayStation, which she referred to as PS in short. She explained that it was an extra one she had, and that she would show Halkano how to play games on it. On the desk there were also brand new Class Eight textbooks, and a new flowery school leather backpack. Halkano moved closer to the laptop and ran her hand over the new keyboard, fearfully at first and treating it like a fragile item that could break with just a tap of the fingers, because the laptop was thin like a piece of paper! She turned to the new textbooks and hesitantly opened them, flipping through the crispy new pages. She had never owned even a single textbook of her own. They only had a few old ones owned by her former school library back in the village, which they had shared among numerous other students. Patricia smiled and said to reassure their guest, "this is all yours, Halkano!"

Later in the sitting room Halkano remained quiet, staring at her surroundings. Almost everything she saw was unfamiliar. She had never seen such a large and flat TV, and it was mounted on the wall! There was also a room Pattie called their home library which was lined with ceiling to floor bookshelves, full of different sorts of novels, storybooks and other books. Halkano marveled how her life had changed these past few months.

Two weeks had passed. Patricia dragged Halkano along with her. She told her, "Halkii, its time you made new besties, now that you're living here in Nairobi. You need to be tight with my crew too!"

Vera and Lucy with wide smiles plastered on their faces, walked over to where Halkano was seated with Patricia. The three best friends blew flying kisses at each other's cheeks.

Then Vera as if she couldn't help herself, screamed, voice shrill, "Pattieeee! Oh. My. Gosh! It's been like soooooooo long!" Halkano had met the two girls once before, when they came to see Patricia after they were discharged from Angels, but she still wondered why they all talked like that, sort of staggering their words in an exaggerated way all the time. Patricia smiled back, then sort of bounced out of her chair, and flew straight into Vera's embrace.

Shortly, Halkano waited for Patricia, Lucy, and Vera to see what they would do with the burgers placed before them because there were so many things like mustard, mayonnaise, and many other dips, sauces, and spices on the table Halkano was not familiar with. She always waited and then followed suit. At the Kwelas, she had learnt a lot this way. As Halkano ate her burger, Lucy and Vera threw wary glances at each other, then at Halkano. At one point, the two tried to catch Patricia's eye through side-glances and side-eyes of their own, sending her a signal that they were indeed curious at Patricia's new friend. After Patricia noticed that her friends were acting odd, she did a little explanation which sparked even more curiosity in them. It was the first time they were meeting someone from Marsabit. They could really use this chance to learn about Marsabit County.

At last Halkano found a chance to speak. "My home is very far from here in Nairobi. We live in North Horr in the remote Marsabit County, in Kenya's northern frontier, near the border with Ethiopia. It's mostly arid in North Eastern Kenya," the first sentence from Halkano forced giggles out of the girls' mouths due to her lilting sing-song accent.

Vera said, "Y'all, Ethiopia! Imagine living next to another country. Halkano, that's so like awesome and cool!" Halkano had come to realize that Vera liked talking in what she'd come to learn was an Americanized accent.

Patricia did not laugh at Halkano's accent because she had got used to it. Halkano did not give much attention to the other two giggling girls. She had been taught at Angels of Mercy, that not everything people did or said needed one's attention, and there she was putting it into practice.

Vera's words though of amazement, that Halkano lived next to Ethiopia, emboldened her more and she continued, "My life, though very short, has just been about the struggle to survive and stay in school. I'm from the Borana community, and in my village many girls my age are married off, forcing them to drop out of school. My case was no exception. Young girls like me have to deal with getting circumcised what is called Female Genital Mutilation or FGM in short. Young girls are at risk of being married off at as early as twelve years. Going to school is a luxury because most of the time I'm supposed to be looking for water. Our county is dry almost all the time. It suffers from drought, famine, and water shortage. Other times I'm busy helping Mama repair our *manyatta*. In our culture a well-maintained *manyatta*, earns a woman respect in the community. Our *manyattas* or *dasses* are portable and made of cow dung, clay, dried grass, and wattle sticks. It is a woman's job to build our *dasses* and also dismantle them when migrating in search of pasture or water. Our *manyatta* is very simple." Patricia's friends gestured for Halkano to continue about the *manyatta*.

"It's partitioned into six rooms. Not even rooms but sort of sections. There is the centre room which serves as a sitting room and kitchen with two pillars in the middle—not actually pillars but sectioned off by strings of colourful Masai beads. This sectioning is meant to protect the children from coming near the ever-burning fireplace. On the right of this middle room is a permanently fixed bed for Baba until time for migration, when it is uprooted. On the left of the sitting room, which has the kitchen too, is Mama's bed. My section I share with my younger sister Guyo and the calves of our cows and the kids of the goats. The last section is a store for the cereals and firewood we have managed to save for the famine. Our older brother Galgalo has his own small manyatta in the homestead. We have pit latrines outside where we also have our baths."

Halkano took a deep breath and then continued, "Though we are culturally rich, we do have a very different lifestyle, and I'm trying to get used to this place." This, the other three girls had already noticed and they didn't need to be told. "Even taking the selfies you girls like so much with your phones, scared me at first because I feared having my photo taken. My people believe that it is a taboo to take one's photo. Our tradition and culture demands and dictates that we live a certain way. My Baba though has started becoming modern, and was even just about to build a permanent stone house, install electricity and running water! So it was not as if marrying me off was for the money and other dowry gifts. But I wish his modernity will include shunning these harmful rituals and practises like FGM and child-marriages!" Halkano took a pause for a sip of water and then continued, "Girls, we also have a lot of cultural differences, and for one I find you to be very free with your elders. For example, I couldn't call Pattie's parents by their first names, June and James, as they had requested because in our culture children are not allowed to call anyone older than themselves by their first names. I was really shocked! *Sema* culture shock?" The four girls burst out laughing.

"Why do you believe that it is bad to take someone's photos?" Vera asked.

"Because when you take someone's picture, it is like you are removing their blood, stealing their soul and shadows. But hey, we do have our fun times in the north, like our Lake Turkana Cultural Festival held annually at Loiyangalani which many people of the northern frontier counties attend, including many other fetes, and the camel derby!" Halkano said.

As if to make Halkano more comfortable, the girls giggled, huddled together with Halkano in their middle, turned on the GPS locations on their smart-phones, and snapped a group selfie.

By the time Halkano finished, Vera and Lucy were looking at her with respect, and yet shock in their eyes at the same time, for they were beginning to realise that what they think is cool, may not always be the most valuable thing in life for others.

THIRTEEN

Patricia was in deep thought. All she remembered was Tony handing her a glass of fruit punch, after they had eaten some food. She did not remember seeing him put anything else into the drink. Maybe the boys had added the drug when her back was turned for a minute, or when she went to the washroom. Or when she took a break from the dancing and went outside to join in the ritual of burning their year eight books to signify clearing primary school. Or when she joined the other students to autograph one another's yearbooks, autograph books, school blouses, trousers, skirts, and shirts with colourful permanent marker pens. Patricia could just not be sure. It was only later that she had felt the drink really hit her hard, and she then became dizzy.

Yesterday Patricia, Halkano, Vera and Lucy, had gone hiking and had a picnic at the nature trail in Oloolau Forest, just a short walk away from the complex. The nature trail which had a picnic site, caves, campsites and an awesome waterfall had relaxed her. But now Patricia was having a bad feeling about the court hearing the following day. It had taken her weeks to be able to say the boy's names out loud. Even now she stuttered and gulped, her voice caught in her throat in a stammer, just trying to say the three names even to herself, "To – n–y, Ia–n, Ar–th–ur." Anxiety filled her, and it felt like it wanted to burst through her chest.

Finally Patricia blurted out, "*Yaani*, can you imagine those *tu*-boys are all still insisting they are not guilty? Cowards!"

"What did you expect, Pattie? That they will just own up and say 'Guilty as charged. We raped her!" Lucy said, exasperated.

Patricia responded, "Lucy, I didn't expect anything! I just wanted them to speak the truth and admit they raped me and then ran away from the party, not keep insisting that I'm lying!" Then she scrolled through her phone and said, "Imagine it's all over the news on the tabloid gutter internet websites like *Uhondo.com* and *Udaku.com*. Here, have a look." Vera and Lucy closed in and peered over Patricia's shoulder.

Patricia, her face crestfallen, voice shaky, added, "Oh no! Can this suck any worse? Look at how they're putting it. Then read the comments section. Imagine one person here is commenting and saying that my IG posts and photos suggest I liked vibing with the boys. Another one says that on the night of the party, I brought the rape upon myself because I was drunk, and must have been dressed provocatively! Yet one more person who doesn't even know me, says I asked for it!"

Vera said, "My mom says we should not read this trash. But it's not only the gutter internet. It's also in this national newspaper, too. It's because your family is well known. Here see,"

Patricia snatched the paper from Vera, and turned to the page she was pointing at. Patricia read through it, "they make it sound like I'm to blame, yet it was your fault, Lucy!" then shouted, looking at Lucy and pointing at her in anger

"Wow! Slow down on the rage, Pattie. You know we got you girl!" Vera said, knowing she had to play peace-maker between her two friends. But it was the wrong thing to say because Patricia turned around in even more intense anger and said, "Yeah! You know what, Vera? I suck because I allowed myself to get raped at that party! I don't know why I even went to that party in the first place. I just vaguely remember going up the stairs to Lucy's bedroom that night! What am I going to tell those boys' lawyer when he starts cross-examining me?" She paused briefly before continuing, "Imagine I'll have to face my three rapists tomorrow, and I honestly just don't want to see them!" Patricia yelled.

"Girl, I sure do hope you soon remember more than just climbing those stairs, or those lover boys are gonna walk free! Remember the CCTV obtained from my house, shows you going up the stairs with them," Lucy said. Lucy's words stung and had a lightning-like effect on Patricia. Patricia sat bolt up-right in her chair with amazing speed. "What else should I remember? I've been having blackouts, and sometimes I forget some details! What do you think the prosecutor will ask me? Oh God! Why did my parents insist on pressing charges? And can you stop going on and on about that damn CCTV?"

"Like how the three boys you've accused, actually *raped* you?" Lucy said, side-stepping Patricia's comment about the CCTV.

"Lucy, don't say the word raped like that. Like I made this up. After all, you are the one who invited those older boys to the party!" Patricia said.

Vera sighed. Her peace-making efforts were hardly bearing fruits.

"I'm sorry, Pattie," Lucy said. "I didn't mean to sound so harsh. Please forgive me. And I've so like blocked all those boys on my social, and call-barred them on my phone!" she added.

The three girls were silent for a long moment.

"Pattie, now I know I should have initially listened to you, about not inviting those boys to the party in the first place. But you know I got cold feet and uninvited them and their friends, but they still gate-crashed. And I regret it!" Lucy then said to Patricia with guilt flitting across her face. She added, "I'm so sorry, Pattie," How could Lucy ever apologize thoroughly and truly to her best friend?

"I'm really, really, so sorry, Pattie. But we do have your back on this!" Lucy repeated for lack of anything better to say. She needed some time alone to also think and she asked out loud, "How could a simple party have gone so terribly wrong? "

The girls strolled in the garden for some time in total silence, just listening to the soothing bird song of cooing doves and pigeons. Lulu barked, her short, sharp, high-pitched sound, and the fluffy poodle happily ran in between the girl's legs.

"It's about time I learnt not to trust every Tom, Dick, and Harry who pretends to be good friends with me," Lucy added for lack of anything else to say, because Patricia was still silent after her last outburst aimed at Lucy. Thankfully they were all huggers sharing spontaneous, loving embraces all the time. They huddled together and embraced in a group hug.

They went back to the patio in the backyard of Patricia's house. Halkano stood to the side, silently watching them. She missed her bestie Misrat, but was now getting used to Patricia's friends. Halkano was also not a hugger. She always felt herself tighten and recoil whenever any of these girls tried to hug her. Maybe it was because of what she had gone through. She watched as Vera and Lucy both hugged a sobbing Patricia and covered her in their warm circle. When they at last moved apart, Patricia's eyes were swollen but she looked calmer.

Vera said, "*Woisheee*! Pattie, we're truly very sorry. I feel so terrible. I had no idea you felt this bad. We love you!"

"How would you know, when I've been refusing to talk to you, my two best friends? I could barely face what I went through, and admit it to myself, until I went to Angels where I met Halkano," Patricia replied.

"That's what your mother told us. That both you and Halkano were really brave to have finished your therapy. It's such an awesome accomplishment! I'm so proud of you two. And Halkano, we're so glad you're now part of our crew. Let your bright shine once more, girls!" Lucy said.

When Lucy and Vera were about to leave, Vera said, "y'all, let's do the mall *kesho*," Then to lighten up the moment she added, "and Pattie, no itchy fingers then, or you might end up in mall jail seeing as we shall be all alone with no adults!" They all laughed, including Halkano, whom Patricia had told about the lip-gloss incident at Karen Mall.

After their two friends had left, Patricia looked away into the distance and said to Halkano, "I don't know about being brave. How come we didn't fight off our rapists? How come we let this happen to us?" Fresh tears sprang to her eyes. "I don't feel brave but helpless." Patricia spoke as if she were talking only with herself.

Halkano covered Patricia's hand with her own, and gave it a gentle squeeze. "We were brave, for it takes bravery to speak up as we were taught at Angels. It takes even more bravery to report to the police, and file a court case as you have done, Pattie. Cheer up. Let's now focus on being positive. After all, you were drugged and raped by three boys so it's not your fault you couldn't fight them off! I think I'm worse off because I still can't even remember fully what happened to me—classic trauma is what Doctor Bilal called it. Classic!" They both burst out laughing at the same time that *Nairobi* also blasted from loudspeakers of a *matatu*, passing behind the highway just beyond the estate's perimeter wall. Mayonde and Stonee Jiwe reminding them about laughter, happiness and loving their city.

Halkano promised Patricia that she would accompany her and her parents to the court hearing to support her. They both agreed that even as much as it was upon them to learn to live with their ordeals, those around them too, had to change in the way they viewed sexual assault.

Patricia suddenly said, "Halkii, I've always wanted siblings. It's no fun being an only child! And I'm so happy you've become like the sister I never had."

Halkano smiled, a wide stretching of her lips, "Pattie, I do miss my brother and sister, but I'm so happy I've gotten another Guyo in you!" They both laughed.

The two girls went back to podding sugar snap peas, and sorting rice for dinner on *uteo* reed trays, a chore they had been helping Selina with, before Lucy and Vera arrived. Mrs Kwela wanted to try for her lemon and butter pea recipe, the new sugar snap peas, a cross between snow and garden peas. But Patricia's mind soon wandered to her lawyer's words a day ago about being consistent before the judge tomorrow. Patricia kept thinking about her lawyer's words…be consistent…but she felt that she might not be consistent as it was hard because of her constant memory lapses of that night's events. She felt she should not be judged on the consistency of her statement, because she had been drugged and even now sometimes couldn't remember some details. She'd overheard her lawyer talk to her parents that consistency was a common test of credibility in court…his words kept ringing in her mind…and she kept wondering, what if she was not consistent? What then? It was like the adults in her life wanted her to cram and memorise her statement which was hard. What Patricia nowadays called her lawyer's and parent's five C's kept echoing in her head… choices…consent…consequences…clarity…consistency… and she now wanted to add another C for conflict, because she felt that was where she was headed with her folks. But she wondered about this consent thingy, because Halkano had said no to dropping out of school, being circumcised and married off, but her parents had not listened to her! Patricia herself had said no to the three boys, but they had still gone ahead and raped her! But because of all this, Patricia knew she had to speak out. She remembered the session she had discussed with Dr Bilal, Jane the Counsellor's three S's of shame, silence and survivor's guilt. Dr Bilal had told her that silence was for the unconcerned, and that she should speak up and out when it mattered, because sometimes due to not voicing concerns, silence too was violence. So now Patricia was learning to overcome all the three S's Jane talked about, and replace them with six of her own; stand up, speak out, set her sights, take up space, there to stay, and slay in her education. Patricia knows she has to start trusting herself, for ever since the rape, not trusting herself, had sort of become her comfort zone maybe because she was still feeling fragile and vulnerable. She's made up her mind to let go her fear, start trusting herself again and not be afraid to exist in any space.

The state prosecutor greeted them all before training his eyes on Patricia. His ceaseless blinking seemed to warn that there was no time to waste. They were seated in a room with the judge and their parents, and not in a courtroom with a dock or witness stand. Patricia took the cue and began searching in her mind.

"Patricia," the prosecutor began like they were all just settling in for a pleasant conversation over a cup of tea, "I have gone through your statement thoroughly but I would like you to walk us through that night again. Tell us what happened from the time you entered Lucy's house, to the minute you ended up at the Karen Hospital. Take as long as you need. We are not in any rush. If I need any clarification, I'll ask you at the end or I might interrupt now and then as we go along."

"Why do I need to go over all that again? Can't you just read aloud to everyone what is in my statement? I signed it, didn't I?" Patricia asked restlessly.

"I know Patricia. But we discussed this, and your lawyer was present. You know you have to narrate the events of that night here again, for the sake of consistency," the prosecutor said gradually.

Patricia stiffened up in her chair, as if conscious for the first time of the people in the room. "Okay. I got to the party at the time when most of the other students were also just arriving—"

The prosecutor put up his hand to interrupt her. "Start at the beginning. I mean right from your friend who invited you to the party. Didn't you have concerns about older boys not from your school being invited—?"

The defence lawyer from the boy's side shot to his feet. "Your Honour, I think that's uncalled for, that is leading the witness!"

The judge looked at the prosecutor over the rim of his eye glasses and said, "He's right. Don't lead the witness. She gave a voluntary statement. She should know what she wants to say here today. Just remember that this is not a full court hearing."

The prosecutor nodded at Patricia. "Take it from there."

Patricia hesitated. She remembered her lawyer's words. *Stick to your story. Be consistent. Consistency is crucial in court, especially in rape and sexual assault cases. Don't start changing things. Your testimony in court has to be the same as your statement.* She began from the beginning. From the day Lucy invited her to the party. She talked for a full fifteen minutes, before coming to the actual rape. Her tongue got heavy and she stopped talking. Her mind silently reviewed the horrible night.

She remembered staggering into the room. There was a bed. A bookshelf. A desk with a laptop. A walk-in wardrobe. Her head hurt. She had sat on the bed. The boys had sat next to her. The one called Tony had moved even closer and leaned into her. He'd kissed her. She was startled and moved away, but the other boys crowded in even closer. She'd felt someone's fingers open her denim jacket's buttons. But she was so groggy. She remembered thinking, 'Why am I so dazed yet I haven't drunk any alcohol? Have I been drugged?' She remembered her parents warning about going to unauthorized parties, or drinking stuff that had not been opened in her presence even at the mall. She'd said goodnight to her parents but later sneaked out of the house through her bedroom window balcony, climbed down the jacaranda tree, and out the backyard gate, and walked the five minutes in the estate to Amboseli complex and to Lucy's. Vera lived at Aberdare complex just a block down the road. Patricia was now lying on the bed and someone was on top of her. Then a mouth on hers, forcing her lips open. Then more hands in between her legs, probing and pushing. They were inside her panties. The person was breathing hard. She tried to pull her face away from him.

"No! Stop! Please stop! I said no! Can't you hear me? Listen to me! No!" She sounded feeble and weak. She heard sounds from faraway like an echo. Sounds of zippers opening. Heavy breathing. Panting. The rustling of clothes. Hands fumbled and slithered her panties off. She soon realized she was naked. Suddenly she saw his face above her. Tony. Strong knees pushed her legs apart. What was happening scared her, but she had no strength to kick him away. She seemed to be moving in slow motion. Then the shocking pain. Lots of pain because she was a virgin. Piercing pain. She lifted her hands to his shoulders and tried to push him off but her hands fell on the bed. Weak. All her limbs were numb and lacked strength. She could not defend herself. She couldn't even summon the strength to get off the bed. Then someone else was on top of her. Ian's face loomed over hers. More intense pain between her legs. They were raping her. Oh God! She opened her mouth and tried to scream but no sound came out. The pain was so bad. She heard voices, 'Just do it, man! Fast!', 'It's your turn dude! Quick!', 'Come on! Kwani are you scared? Do it then!' The third boy was now on top of her. It was Arthur. She could make out his pale, light face. His full weight was suffocating her. Patricia thought she was going to die from the pain and from suffocating. She could not breathe and felt helpless. Finally Arthur rolled off her. Suddenly she was alone in the room. They were gone. She vomited on the bed. She stayed still for a long moment, motionless. Reality dawned that she was on the first floor in Lucy's bedroom.

Finally, she got up and struggled to put on her clothes. She staggered down the stairs, holding onto the banister and then collapsed at the foot of the stairwell. She was sobbing hysterically. All she remembered was screaming that she'd been raped. Lucy called their immediate neighbours, a middle-aged couple who ordered all the young people to leave, and said the party was over. Then the short drive to the Karen Hospital. Patricia remembered Vera talking to Lucy while they waited for her to finish undergoing her medical exam. "OMG! Lucy! I told you I had a bad feeling about this party," Vera told Lucy. She was holding her stomach and rocking back and forth like she was in terrible pain. "What are we going to tell Pattie's parents? Mine will never let me leave the house alone again. Ever! I'll be grounded for like forever!"

Patricia's parents had arrived at the hospital in shock... The police had been called and arrived from the Karen Police Station...A P3 form had been filled...later Patricia had given her statement to the female police officer.

Patricia came back to earth and to the present in the courthouse, in the judge's private chamber. She found her voice again and finished narrating as if in a trance. Her lawyer took over from the prosecutor.

"You were all drinking some sort of punch?"

Patricia looked at her parents who gave her the thumbs-up sign. She nodded slowly. "Yes, but the fruit punch I took was non-alcoholic."

"Do you remember how many glasses you took of this cocktail, punch, or whatever drink it was?"

"I took a couple of tumblers before Tony brought me a third glass."

Her lawyer looked at her statement and wrote something in his notepad. "Do you remember how you felt after drinking this third glass given to you by Tony? Were you clear-headed or dizzy?"

"Very tired. I remember finding it strange that I suddenly felt dazed, woozy and kinda groggy," Patricia said softly.

"If you were asked to rate your clarity of mind on a scale of one to ten, with one being completely alert and ten being unconscious, where on this scale would you rate yourself at that time during the party after drinking from the glass given to you by Tony?"

"Nine or maybe even ten."

There were gasps, murmurs, and collective sighs of shock in the room, from the family members and friends present.

"Do you remember what happened next?"

"I found the boys crowding me and we were going up the stairs, and into Lucy's bedroom. It was just a few minutes later that I realized they were all raping me."

More shocked gasps from the room. Patricia's lawyer said he rested his case.

The boy's lawyer addressed the Judge and said, "Your Honour, I would like to cross-examine the complainant."

The Judge, using his index finger, pushed his spectacles which had slid further down the bridge of his nose upwards and said, "You may, Counsel."

The boy's lawyer started, "Patricia, do you remember the three boys who you claim raped you?"

"Yes. I do remember three of them and it was Tony, Arthur and Ian."

"Are they in this room right now?"

"Yes. There they are." Patricia pointed at the three boys who were seated together on one bench. "Tony is the one in the middle with the checked shirt. Arthur is the pointy! Sorry, I mean the half-caste one to his left. And Ian is the one seated to Tony's right-hand side."

Arthur blushed a deep red and dropped his head, when Patricia pointed at him and said the words pointy and half-caste, which referred to a person of mixed race of African and white.

"Tell me something about this drink Tony gave you. You said that you felt groggy after drinking it. How then were you able to identify these three, from among all the boys who were at that party that night? And haven't you been experiencing blackouts and memory loss, as you claimed from your statement due to the so-called drug that was used to spike your drink? How then are you now all of a sudden very clear about things?"

"I remember them because they were the ones who crowded me on the stairs, and led me to Lucy's room. They were all drunk and rowdy, too," Patricia replied confidently.

"You all live in the same estate. Are you friends with these boys? You follow each other on all social media don't you? You and your girlfriends Lucy and Vera, and my three clients are tight on social media as you young people say. Tight! And haven't you shared photos of yourself in your bikini, on your Instagram for them to see? And didn't you tell some of your girlfriends that you think my clients are cute? That you wouldn't mind having one of them as your boyfriend?" The lawyer's voice was now loud, rushed and hurriedly piling the questions one right after another, pointing at Patricia one minute and the next pivoting on his heels and pointing at the three boys in a dramatic way.

Patricia shook her head fiercely. "No. They aren't my friends! I just see them at church, around the estate, at swimming galas, the Karen Mall, or the community centre, and occasionally places like the Giraffe Centre. We might be friends on our social, but my photos were not for them! I also didn't tell any of my besties that I wanted a boyfriend, how dare you lie!" She stood and was shouting.

"Do you remember seeing Patrick at the party? That's Patrick over there." The lawyer, unfazed, though at Patricia's raised voice, changed tact and pointed at Patrick. "He will take the stand shortly. And remember, we also have CCTV footage obtained from Lucy's house, and it shows you willingly went up the stairs, and that's the reason why my clients, the three defendants, Arthur, Tony and Ian, maintain their not guilty plea. The sex was consensual!"

Patricia sat down with a heavy plop and said, "No, I don't remember seeing Patrick. The party was crowded, and the room was getting darker and darker," her voice was suddenly not confident anymore, "And the reason I went up the stairs is because they had drugged me! They raped me! It wasn't consensual!"

The lawyer pounced again, "But you very clearly seem to remember Tony, Ian, and Arthur. Very strange because Patrick was at that party too, and he doesn't remember seeing the three boys drunk or rowdy. Now I'm really fascinated by this third glass of some punchy concoction that you claim Tony gave you. In your statement, you say that you suspect he laced or spiked your drink with some drug? How sure are you that it was not the overall fruit punch you all at the party had already taken, that was drugged? Did you actually see Tony, Ian or Arthur, drug your drink? And how do we know that you really didn't want to have sex with these boys?

I declare you are lying about everything, young lady!" the lawyer shouted at Patricia.

Patricia burst into tears. Her mother rushed to her side with a box of tissues. She dabbed her daughter's face and nose, but Patricia continued sobbing, tears streamed down her face.

"Why are you letting him ask my baby such difficult questions? And why is he calling her a liar? He's upset her!" Patricia's mother shouted at the judge. Everyone in the room started talking all at the same time.

"How dare you speak of rape, Patricia? *Si* it was consensual? And you agreed to it!" Tony stood up and shouted at Patricia.

The judge looked at the boys' lawyer and said, "Control your clients. Ask them to remain silent until they take the stand."

"I didn't agree to anything, Tony! I wasn't even in my senses because you'd drugged me with Rope!" Patricia screamed back.

The judge agreed with Patricia's mother and said, "I'm sorry about that, Mrs Kwela, you're right, and Patricia is clearly very upset. Let's take ten. Just a short break."

Later the judge adjourned the case till the next day.

The following day, after the judge turned his attention to the boy's lawyer, the latter said, "My clients won't be taking the stand, and that is not to say that they have pleaded guilty. No, they haven't."

Only Patrick took to the stand as a witness for Arthur, Ian and Tony. He categorically stated that the boys were not drunk, neither were they rowdy. He also said to Patricia's dismay, that he didn't see the three boys anywhere near her on the night of the party.

It was a week later.

Ian flopped onto the couch. They had just taken a group selfie, smiling and trying to cheer themselves up but he still felt terrible. His other two co-accused friends had come out to hang at Ian's house in Shimba Hills complex. It was a consolation though, to notice that Tony looked worried and visibly shaken.

"I hear the judgement is tomorrow," Arthur started calmly.

Ian lowered his head into his hands, sighed, and let out a timid groan like a distressed kitten purring. "Oh no! Not so soon. I'm legit worried about this case now! We might end up in juvy!" he said referring to juvenile prison.

Arthur shot up straight from his seat and stood stiffly like a bullet had just pierced his back. "Yes, Dad told me. But he also said you guys don't need to worry, that everything will be alright."

The two boys looked at him in relief and then Tony spoke, "Arthur, you should know. After all your father is the deputy DPP!"

Ian moved closer to where Arthur was standing. "What exactly did he tell you, Arthur? *Si* you just tell us!"

"Sorry, dude. I can't talk about it. I promised Dad I'll keep my mouth shut. You'll find out tomorrow," Arthur answered back calmly.

"Yo! Dude! We know you must have promised," Tony said eagerly. "But man, this is us. Come on, dude! We're asking as friends. After all we're in the same boat. This will stay here in this house. It will remain between us."

Arthur moved towards the main front door and said, "Relax! *Msikonde!*" The Kiswahili slang literally means don't grow thin, but figuratively means not to worry.

Arthur added, "anything you want to find out, you'll know tomorrow. Just take a chill pill for now. I assure you it ain't too elephant!" Arthur used the Kenyan-speak to refer to something big and serious.

"*That's it? Is that all you're gonna tell us?*" Ian sounded annoyed but Arthur was already at the front door and said, "meet later at church? Remember the youth pastor said he wants to talk to us about joining the basketball team, now that we're done with school and no longer on the school team. And also about being more active in the youth group. *Form ni ku-hustle.*" Arthur went out the door before Ian and Tony could respond.

Ian heard a new track playing with great trap lyrics, from the home theatre in the corner of the sitting room. It was Kiss FM but the presenter had already introduced the song. Ian said, "Tony, these lyrics are dope! Is it a new song?"

Tony replied, "Ian, *si* you just Shazam it?" Tony was referring to the Apple app that identifies music and even movies, based on a short sample played and using the microphone on one's phone so long as it's near the source of the sound.

Ian laughed and hit his forehead with his open palm, "Silly me! Of course!" he quickly clicked on the Shazam app icon on his phone and slid it near the home theatre's speaker, before the song ended. The app within five seconds identified the lyrics and rapper, and played it. Ian quickly saved the track to his playlist.

FOURTEEN

Halkano reluctantly wore the skinny jeans with trendy tear at the knees, and fancy blouse with open patches at the shoulders, Pattie had given her. It was her first time wearing a pair of trousers, and they gave her a feeling between comfort and embarrassment. The jeans, however, fit her almost perfectly because she was just about the same size, weight, and height as Pattie. Halkano looked at herself in the full-length mirror in Patricia's room. She did look good! Her hair was starting to grow back because here at the Kwelas, she did not have to shave it. Yesterday they had both gone to the salon; Halkano got her hair shampooed, conditioned, treated, and blow-dried, while Patricia had her dreadlocks washed, moisturised, treated, and re-twisted.

Patricia now moved Halkano to her side, and showed her how to tilt her head to the right, and how to preen and prance about, looking at herself from different Angels.

Ten minutes later, at the Karen Mall, Halkano stared when the automatic glass doors slid open as Patricia and her mother neared the entrance. Halkano quickly slipped inside too, fearing the sliding doors would lock her outside. A female security guard threw a surprised look her way.

Halkano laughed at herself when Patricia explained to her that the mall's main entrance doors had sensors, which could tell when people approached.

Later they bought some delicious Fro-Yo to eat, and Patricia told Halkano Fro-Yo was short for frozen yoghurt. They also had ice-cream cake and pizza, things Halkano had never eaten in her fourteen years of life. Each time she tasted something she had not eaten before, she tilted her nose as if to get the proper aroma and ate slowly as if to savour and save the taste in her mouth.

Patricia's mother bought Halkano several pairs of jeans, beautiful skirts, blouses, ankle-length boots, sneakers, and comfortable, flat doll shoes, schoolbags, a handbag, a tiny leather backpack like Patricia's that was currently in fashion, and many other items.

Patricia also started selecting clothes off hooks and hangers and put them in her trolley.

"Pattie," Mrs Kwela said, "We're here to shop for Halkano and not you! You have so many new clothes in your wardrobe you've not even worn! No more. What you've picked is enough for today!"

"Cool," Pattie replied. The ease with which Patricia obeyed the order surprised Mrs Kwela. How her daughter had changed.

Halkano was surprised because Patricia's mother paid for everything they bought using different cards she got from her wallet, which the cashiers swiped at a small machine.

Halkano was fascinated when they entered a glass sort of box, whose door closed on them with other shoppers inside and Pattie pressed a number on the side of the box. When it started moving, Halkano almost stumbled. She later clung onto one of the rails by the sides. The box moved at a fast speed going upwards, and Halkano looked at the other floors through the transparent glass sides of the box, as the different storeys flashed past.

When Patricia noticed Halkano's eyes enlarge, she said, "It's taking us to another floor. This machine is called an elevator." A smile formed on Halkano's lips, as if laughing silently at herself.

Afterwards, they used some steps which just slid like a long belt being pulled by some mysterious, hidden force. Halkano kept trying to walk on it trying to balance herself, but she almost slid off.

"This is called an escalator," Patricia said, trying not to smile at her friend's fright. "Don't walk on it. Just hold to the railing and stand still. It will move us along."

By the time they were done visiting a couple more floors, and shopping on all the five floors of the mall at shops Halkano learnt were called designer outlets, the rope handles on the shopping bags were digging her hands but Halkano did not mind. It was her first shopping trip for brand new clothes at a mall, and the red painful welts in the middle of her palms were like her hard-earned badges of honour from her Girl-Guide troop at her old school, and how happy she felt when Mama was proud after seeing the water she had fetched from the pan, and brought back home with her little sister Guyo. Halkano was so humbled by Mrs Kwela's generosity.

The cathedral looked imposing with the stained colourful windows that glinted in the sunlight. The sexton tolled the bell hanging from the belfry and the melodic hymns reverberated from the church. Mrs Kwela dipped her fingers into the holy water and made the sign of the cross. Her family followed behind through the central column to a pew upfront.

Halkano trailed Patricia and her parents into the cathedral. She followed suit and touched the water in the small ceramic sink attached to the wall near the main entrance. Halkano also knelt and closed her eyes and started praying. The parish was teeming with Catholic faithful. The aroma of spiritual incense and whiffs of smoke teased the nostrils. The congregants were looking forward to celebrating Holy Communion. The shiny purple hue of the Father's Papal-blessed ring, glinted in the morning light as he made the sign of the cross.

Halkano had already learnt and memorized a few Hail Mary's, and she recited a few silently in her heart. *Oh, Mother of Mercy, Mother of penitent sinners, I stand before you sinful and sorrowful, beseeching you through the immense Love given to you by the Holy Spirit for us poor sinners...Oh Virgin Mary, My Mother, through that ineffable Wisdom bestowed upon you by the Incarnate Word of God, I humbly beseech you, obtain for me Meekness and humility of heart ...*

Halkano had fallen in love with the cathedral's architecture. The church was beautiful and in the shape of a cross. The aisle was lined with opaque glass of different texture and stained colours and it led to the altar. At the raised altar, there was a table covered with a spotless white lacy material with Holy Communion stuff already laid out. The statue of Mother Mary cradling baby Jesus in her arms, always reminded Halkano of her mother, especially when she was missing her family. Halkano followed suit every time the congregants bowed or knelt on the soft, maroon cushions, placed beside their pews.

"*Mother, you are watching me. Please guide us, your children,*" Halkano prayed just like she had heard Patricia pray before.

The middle-aged Father dressed in a white and green robe, with gold embroidered front, walked up the aisle towards the altar. The usual group of young girls in white tee-shirts and colourful *leso* skirts led the procession, singing and dancing. The Father holding his chalice with incense smoke billowing from it, blessed the faithful by sprinkling holy water on them. The people responded by making the sign of the cross. The Father accompanied by three altar boys dressed in white vestments, went behind the altar. The catechist with incense holder and Bible in his hand was already at the altar. Behind him was the choir in their purple and white flowing uniforms.

The choir sang a few hymns with the congregation. The sermon was brief on this day. Soon Mass was over. "*God be with you,*" the Father said and made the sign of the cross. "*And with you too, Father,*" the congregation chorused. Soon it was the Kwela's turn to receive Sacrament. Halkano stared at the Father who was now seated, as the seminarian with the assistance of the altar boys took the goblets. The Father stood at the altar and made the final sign of the cross. He led the procession from the altar through the middle aisle of the pews. Outside, the Kwela family took their turn to shake the Father's hand. "*Christ the Kingdom come, Father.*" Halkano followed Patricia's actions and extended her right hand towards the Father. The Father told them, "*God bless you. God be with you, my children,*" Halkano responded, "*And also with you, Father.*"

Halkano was learning fast about Palm Sunday, Ash Wednesday, and Lent, among other Catholic special days. And she too was teaching Patricia about her Islam celebrations and special months and like Ramadhan, Maulidi which is Prophet Muhammad's birthday, and Eid ul Fitr the festival of purification after finishing the holy fasting month of Ramadhan. Mrs Kwela had promised Halkano, that they would help her during Ramadhan for the full month of fasting which would soon be upon them, by making sure that her meals were prepared on time. Patricia had learnt that Ramadhan meant observing *Sawm* the fasting, for thirty days, and abstaining from food between sunrise and sunset for the full lunar month. And that *Sawm* begins at sunrise during the *Fajr* prayer before dawn, and is broken at sunset preceding the *Maghreb Salat*, which is the fourth prayer. And so Mrs Kwela promised that the meal served before sunrise called the *Suhoor*, and the one to break the fast after sunset called *Iftar*, would always be ready for Halkano.

After church and a lunch treat at Pizza Place at the Karen Mall and once home, the girls rushed up to Halkano's room. Halkano still had so much to learn. Patricia's parents smiled and watched, as the girls ran up the stairs excitedly, almost tripping on the carpeted steps.

"Nowadays my favourite app is Snapchat because unlike IG, I can send my friends photos and videos and the images disappear a few seconds after someone has viewed them!" Patricia began the lesson. "I'll download that one for you too," she told Halkano who was concentrating hard not to miss what Patricia was teaching her. Halkano had been baffled by this thing called the internet. The fact that one could do or read things by just searching on this internet thing had left her bewildered. And as if that was not enough, one could access it all over the house, whichever room one was in, even in the washroom! Patricia told her that this invisible internet was called Wi-Fi.

Halkano had thought that the phone Patricia's parents had bought her was only for calling her family and bestie Misrat. Halkano knew about Facebook from the single cyber cafe at their local market in Marsabit, and of course at school people talked about Facebook but she never thought she would one day have her own social media accounts. The previous day, they had already downloaded WhatsApp from the phone's app store, and Patricia had already added her to the family group.

Patricia chattered excitedly. "Unlike sending photos or text messages in other apps, Snapchat allows you to set a one-second to ten-second expiration of the photo or video, that way you need not worry that someone will steal it and do naughty stuff with it or share it with other people on other platforms." Halkano, who was the student, just did the listening.

Patricia said, "There! I've downloaded it. Come and register and set a password. Always use one you can remember, like the one you started using on Facebook yesterday. Cool! Now all you need to do is add new friends you might meet. You can already add me, Lucy, and Vera. Here, let me show you how to search for us so that you can add us."

"Cool!" Halkano said and they both burst out giggling. However, Halkano's giggling stopped almost immediately as she resumed a still and composed posture.

A month had passed since Halkano went to live with Patricia's family in Nairobi. Life was so different when she compared the leafy Karen suburb where the Kwela's lived, to the dry and dusty Marsabit, so much so that Halkano wondered if Marsabit County was even part of Kenya. Here they had running water from taps in every room. The family now even had a chauffeur who drove the girls whenever they wanted to go somewhere for games, or weekends when Patricia's parents were not home to drive them.

Halkano was happy because she knew she was safe from her father. However, there were days when she wished she could go back home and visit her brother Galgalo, sister Guyo, and bestie Misrat. On such days she made every effort to hide her loneliness from Patricia and her parents, her efforts included lying on her back on the lawns in the backyard garden. Sometimes she pretended to be feeling unwell, and locked herself in her room where she collapsed on the bed and sobbed quietly. And it was never just missing them, especially for Guyo. She had been worried about what would become of Guyo, until she heard that Patricia's parents had offered to accommodate both of them. She looked forward to the day when her sister would join her.

"Halkano, we know you have been worried about your sister," Mrs Kwela started at the dinner table one evening.

"We have considered the possibility of bringing Guyo here too. Everything will be well," Mr Kwela assured her.

Patricia's parents and their lawyer were working on the paperwork to also in addition to Halkano, to become Guyo's legal guardians too, because their mother was only out on bail and there was an impending jail sentence hanging over her head for colluding with her husband to marry of their daughter. News had also reached the Kwelas that Halkano's father and Sasura, were also waiting to be sentenced for their part in the child-marriage case. Galgalo had just turned eighteen and said he would take care of himself as he was now adult. It had then been decided that there was no need for a guardian for him. When Halkano's mother visited the Kwela's before her sentencing, Halkano was overjoyed. She had hovered around her mother who was dressed in a new flowing, colourful, silk dera dress, *bui bui* and matching *hijab.* The natural red *henna,* and black *piko* in beautiful, flowery motifs which had been painted on her feet for Halkano's wedding to Sasura a couple of months ago were fading. Halkano had learnt that henna application has rules. For example, a married woman applies *henna* on her feet, while an unmarried woman decorates her hands. There are exceptions though, in that married women can be allowed to apply *henna* on their hands on very special occasions.

"They are so good to me. Patricia treats me like her own sister and so do her parents," Halkano finally announced to her mother.

"We are going to make this day memorable," Mrs Kwela told Halkano's mother.

The Kwelas invited for dinner, the neighbours and other guests, among them the Angels of Mercy family including Doctor Bilal, Jane the counsellor, and Christine the head nurse.

"It is worth a celebration," Mr Kwela remarked.

As all sat in the sitting room, Halkano's mother narrated what had happened back at home after the police had gone to arrest her, Halkano's father and Sasura, for marrying Halkano off.

"Mama, we should be grateful to the Kwelas. Now I will continue with my education uninterrupted," Halkano said just before her mother started speaking.

Everyone kept quiet to listen to Halkano's mother.

"...after we were released from police custody on bail, pending the hearing, a communal hearing was convened. Halkano, you were the one being tried in absentia. They had decided as a community not to allow the police charges against your husband Sasura, your father, and myself to proceed. Instead, the village elders convened the usual traditional court. Food was served. People celebrated at our traditional court, as a way of cleansing the curse of a girl daring to conspire with the police to arrest and take to court her parents, and maybe even have them jailed. It is *mwiko*." Taboo.

If anyone had heard Halkano say these things and not believed, that was the time they put their doubts aside. Halkano's mother went on, "Halkano had done what was considered an unmentionable and unheard of taboo, just like rape in marriage is unspoken of in our culture. It was a very solemn time for your father and me as the ceremony got underway. The ritual was simple but the elderly men were very bitter with me. They kept saying that I didn't know how to bring up daughters in our traditions."

At the traditional court, village elders had taken turns in admonishing her. "You're a useless woman, wife, and mother! You have not brought up your daughter well. How dare you let your silly girl accuse her husband of rape?"

"Your daughter is a disgrace to this village! How dare she plan with her teachers and the police, to have her husband and parents arrested? She's done something extremely bad and unheard of. She has spoken about matters that are taboo, an abomination, and thus cast a dark cloud on our traditions and our ways!" another elder had added.

The elders had accused Halkano's mother of among other things, soiling their culture.

Halkano's mother said, "Their decision still rings in my head. There is nothing like rape in marriage. Let us not forget the ways of our people. *Mwacha mila ni mtumwa.* Halkano's case is no case at all. She will accept as compensation some money, these cattle, goats, camels, and maize, because our village court has decided so."

That day at the Kwela's dinner, afterwards, Halkano's mother, feeling pensive, kept her head bowed at the table. Halkano sat next to her mother at the table and from time to time, she would check on her through the corner of her right eye. But most of the time, Halkano avoided the eyes of everyone because she was trying to conceal the surging emotions within her, about her mother. Her mother, however, still caught her side-glances. One moment she smiled and reached across the table, and took her daughter's hand and said in Kiswahili, "*Nisamehe mwanangu. Nakupenda sana.*" She smiled to ease the tension. Halkano returned her mother's side-eye, squeezed her hand, and said, "Mama, I forgive you. I love you too."

Mrs Shah, the Kwela's Indian neighbor, who had accompanied her husband, said when Halkano's mother finished talking, "I've heard of these alternative dispute resolution systems steeped in culture and tradition." Everyone shot a glance at her, including Halkano's mother. "Isn't that what some communities in northern Kenya call *Maslaha*, which they apply to resolve various disputes, including cases of rape and defilement, where perpetrators only pay fines in the form of livestock or grain, and occasionally some money?"

No one responded to confirm her statement. But shortly Halkano's mother said, "Yes. That is what it's called. *Maslaha*. Like what happened at our traditional court, concerning Halkano's case."

Dr Bilal cleared his throat like a schoolmaster, about to address a morning assembly at which pupils were murmuring.

"We still have a long way to go when it comes to sexual abuse, especially rape of children. It's good though that the government is really trying hard to entrench equity in social justice." He lowered his voice like someone about to whisper, "in case you did not know, the Sexual Offenses Act has been amended to include attempted rape as an offense. You know sometimes it is more of submission from a victim than consent, as it might be suggested or insinuated in some cases, because the person is scared!"

It was as if the doctor had broken the frigid ice, and given everyone at the table the power to speak.

"I know a lady who was last year raped in a carjacking. Her sister works at my firm. The police told her she must have been drunk, and they recorded the rape in the OB as a robbery with violence," Mr Shah said. He was about to add something but the doctor's voice had already taken over.

"We must not forget that because of the stigma and taboo, some women still go ahead and shower, even though many know that they need to get a post-rape exam within seventy-two hours, and should therefore not bathe before this medical exam." Doctor Bilal said.

"Most victims say they feel much safer and cleaner once they bathe, but by then they have destroyed the evidence! Some don't even know that they need to get vaccinated for hepatitis and given the post-exposure prophylaxis medication usually given to rape victims, to protect them from probable HIV infection," the kindly voice of Jane, the head counsellor at Angels of Mercy, pointed out from the farthest end of the table.

"The lady who works at my office said her sister didn't know how to cope with the trauma and she sunk into depression and became an alcoholic. She was angry all the time, until finally one of their family members forced her to join a restoration program that helped her," Mr Shah added.

Mrs Kwela's face brightened at Mr Shah's words and she said, "Survivors of SGBV say that they need organizations to create sustainable measures that will prevent sexual, and gender-based violence. More hospitals need to better be able to handle sexual assault cases. They need to be equipped with GVRC," she looked at the two young girls seated at the table and added, "that is the acronym for Gender Violence Recovery Centre. And SGBV stands for Sexual and Gender-Based Violence." Halkano and Patricia nodded in comprehension.

In solidarity with his wife, Mr Kwela found his voice, "We should encourage this, and we have agreed as a family, that we shall initiate and register a foundation that gives survivors of sexual abuse and assault who are fragile and vulnerable, a safe refuge and emotional support through counseling, and to create awareness of this violation because many don't know what to do or who to turn to for help."

"Some like our daughter and Halkano here are a little bit luckier because they got the help they needed. We even had DNA proof because Pattie was rushed straight to the hospital without having a bath! We're glad she received the best care at the Karen Hospital. The foundation will also have a youth centre that will sensitise youth against date rape, and spiking of victim's drinks using drugs like Rohypnol, Diazepam, and Ketamine, locally on our streets called mchele. Those boys drugged our Pattie here using Rohypnol. I hear they call it Rope, date rape drug, Bugizi or forget-me pill. I've done some research on this."

Dr Bilal said, "It's very expensive to seek such help, and a subsidized foundation will be of great assistance. The huge financial burden scares many away from seeking professional help, despite the cost co-sharing already in place in public hospitals."

Patricia spoke up, "At least the boys who raped me faced a judge, even if they've been put on community service!"

Mr Kwela looked at his phone and said, "That's about to change! KOT got your backs, girls, you know Kenyans on Twitter. Trending at number one on TwitterKE is #LetsTalkAboutThisRapeCulture. How is that for good news?"

"Yes!" Patricia jumped up and punched her fist into the air, and then turned to Halkano, and fist-bumped and high-fived with her. Halkano responded to the bump and high-five. They crowded around to look at the trending hashtag on Mr Kwela's phone. There was one Twitter user's tweet which had gone viral; she was at a protest march and had posted photos of many people in the crowd who were carrying placards or wearing tee-shirts with slogans which said, 'No' does not mean 'Yes', 'No Consent. No Sex', 'No' does not mean 'Convince me' and 'No' does not mean 'Maybe', and 'No' means 'No!'

FIFTEEN

After the ruling had been issued, and the three boys put on community service, everyone had resumed their lives as if nothing unusual had happened. It was as if the case had not even been there in the first place. But that was not the case for Patrick. While his friends Tony, Ian, and Tony, had taken pride in the cover-up they had perfectly been coached on, rehearsed, and relayed before the court, Patrick's self-criticism did not allow his conscience to let him off so easily. And so in his room when alone, he reprimanded himself in self-indignation. He deemed what he had done immoral and for days, he could not find peace within himself. When the hashtag #LetsTalkAboutThisRapeCulture began to trend on social media and did so for many days, Patrick fell into some kind of trance. Every social network he checked, the name Patricia Kwela popped up, as people questioned what had happened behind the scenes of the case. For days on end, his mother could not convince him to eat his food. Whenever his mother sneaked in to check on him, she found a surly son. The name Patricia Kwela gave him sleepless nights. But what troubled him most was that he had been used as a key determinant in the case. The scene involving him standing at the judge's chamber and lying in defence of his friends, flashed before his eyes. His mother tried to assure him that he was not to blame for how the case went down but to no avail.

"I have no peace," he said to his mother one day when he appeared a little bit revived. "I feel that I have wasted that girl's life," he said when his mother asked him how he felt and what he wanted to do about it.

And still, Patrick's mother tried to give her son a long list of excuses for why he should not blame himself, but it amounted to nothing for Patrick. He could not get it out of his mind.

"Patrick, how are you?" her mother had asked one night.

Patrick closed his eyes.

"Did you hear me, Patrick?"

"Don't worry, Mom."

His mother paced the room up and down, before holding her arms akimbo, and stood still at the head of the bed.

"Patrick, why are you doing this to yourself and to me?"

"Mom, I have told you before that I can't stop thinking about it," he replied.

His mother, as if overwhelmed by the task which lay ahead of going back to the judge with a confession of changing a deceitful statement, which might bring a charge of perjury against her only child, she'd put her palms to her forehead and splayed the fingers over her eyes as if to forget, and closed her eyes for a good long moment as if contemplating such a moment.

When his mother could no longer keep up with his state of mind, one evening she resignedly told him that the following day they would seek peace.

The judge stared over his wide-rimmed spectacles at the young man standing before him. "Patrick, what you are saying is that you want to change your statement. What, if I may ask, brought about this wish?"

Patrick looked at his mother and their new lawyer, who had arranged the meeting with the judge. They both nodded at him to proceed.

"I know that it was wrong, and I'm feeling very guilty for covering up for my friends during the hearing. I've been unable to sleep properly, because my conscience has been troubling me," Patrick said.

"Do you know that you committed a serious offense called perjury?" the judge asked Patrick.

"Yes, sir," Patrick hung his head in shame, "My lawyer here told me about perjury, and I also Googled it. But I agreed with my mom that this is the right thing to do. I'm sorry about lying while under oath."

"And are you aware that you could also go to jail for this offense?" the judge asked just to be sure.

"Yes sir," Patrick replied, though now scared at what the judge's decision might be.

Patrick's mother spoke up at that moment, "Your Honour. I feel as guilty as my son, because initially I encouraged him not to divulge what he knew. I'm also ashamed of myself and I sincerely apologise, because an innocent young girl is being thought of as a liar."

"Good. Patrick, you can proceed with your new statement," the judge said sternly.

Patrick did so shortly when the court stenographer was seated at her steno machine, ready to type and transcribe, and court clerk ready with her recorder.

"I saw the guys spiking some drinks, and they were totally drunk and high on weed. Tony later that week bragged about forcing Patricia to have sex with him, and so did Arthur and Ian. I'm really so ashamed of myself for lying earlier, your Honour."

Patrick took half an hour to explain to the judge the truth that Tony had told him, about what transpired the night of the party and the rape. He then signed a new written statement with the fresh facts.

The following day, Ian's father, aunt, and uncle requested a meeting with the judge, too. Ian also wanted to come clean and retract his not guilty plea, and confess to the rape saying they had been drunk and high on *bangi* that night.

There was a positive turn of events the following month, when Tony's parents who encouraged their son to lie and tried to tamper with evidence, were put under investigation. Arthur's father, the deputy DPP, who had colluded with Tony's parents, had also been indicted, then suspended, and was being investigated by the Ethics and Anti-Corruption Commission (EACC) on corruption charges, and meddling in cases, with the intent to conceal evidence.

Two of Kenya's leading national newspapers had an almost similar headline to the new outcome of the court case: **'TWO RAPES, ONE NATIONAL VERDICT: STOP TURNING A BLIND EYE TO RAPE CULTURE. LET'S TALK ABOUT THIS!'** The reporter went on to detail how a couple of months ago, the Director of Public Prosecutions (DPP) had recalled the two files related to Patricia Kwela and Halkano Abaduba's cases after social media outcry and the cases coming to the public's attention, especially with the Kwela family having taken in Halkano and the foundation that had been initiated. Ian's confession to the rape, and Patrick's about-turn on his real conversation about the rape with Tony and Arthur and Ian's bragging to him had made it possible to recall Patricia's file. The three boys' community service sentences had been changed to three years in juvenile prison, and a subsequent year of probation upon release. They were sentenced as minors because they were all still seventeen, and their eighteenth birthdays which could have seen them tried in court as adults, were still a few months away. Patrick was put on community service for six months for his perjury, and because he was remorseful as the judge noted, he was spared a prison sentence. Halkano's parents and Sasura were jailed for seven years each with no option of a fine. The news articles talked on the positive power of technology and social media, referring to modern young people as tech-digital netizens, saying the impact and meaning of this new generation's online, engaged active citizenship, meant that they could bring lasting positive change to communities, equity, social justice and social protection when used positively.

Patricia took the newspaper they were reading and waved it high above her head, and did a little dance around the room. Halkano stamped her feet, clapped and skipped about the room before turning to embrace Patricia tightly. Then they went to their laptops to Google some more on what people were saying online, about this positive turn in events. The highlight was on the precedent the DPP had made, in recalling the two files. And the other precedent set by the judge, in overturning the earlier rulings.

SIXTEEN

One Friday, Patricia decided to follow Halkano to the local mosque, which was ten minutes' walk from the Kwela's residence. Patricia was fascinated by Halkano's prayers the daily five *Salat* called *Alfajiri, Aduhuri, Alasiri, Maghreb* and *Isha*. Though Halkano giggling yesterday had admitted that sometimes she doesn't pray all five, even though from the Kwela's house, they usually heard the five daily calls of the Muezzin calling the *Adhan* from loudspeakers atop the minarets of the local mosque, urging faithful to pray and go to the mosque calling out, '*Allah u Akbar...La ilhaha... illullah.*" Halkano had told Patricia it meant God is the Greatest, and there is no God but Allah.

"Halkano, you know I've been wondering. I always thought that women and girls are not allowed to go to the mosque. Or if they do go, they have to be accompanied by a male member of the family."

"You're right, Pattie. A long time ago there used to be very strict conditions. But, praise be to Allah, it's now permissible for women to go to the mosque and pray, subject to certain conditions."

As she adjusted her *juzu* and flipped pages of the Quran, Halkano added, "A long time ago, one of these conditions was that a woman had to be accompanied by a maharam, which means a male family member. But this has changed, and it means that there is nothing wrong with her going to the mosque to pray without a maharam, especially now that nowadays a women's section for prayers has been established at all masjids. Here, have a look at this passage here it says in *Fataawa al-Lajnah al-Daa'imah, 7/332.*"

Patricia stared blankly.

Halkano knew that Patricia could not read Arabic, which was the language of the Quran that Patricia's father had bought her. Halkano had been so excited because this was her first Quran. She had been amazed to find out when reading the Bible with Patricia, that the two Holy Books were so similar in many aspects.

But now in the comfort of the laptop in her room and Google, Patricia typed the section of the Quran Halkano had read to her, and opened up a passage.

Patricia started reading the passage. "It is permissible for a Muslim woman to pray in the mosque and her husband does not have the right to stop her if she asks him for permission to do that, so long as she is properly covered and no part of her body is showing that it is forbidden for "strangers" (non mahrams) to see. It was narrated that Ibn 'Umar said: I heard the Messenger of Allah (peace and blessings of Allah be upon him) say: "When your womenfolk ask you for permission to go to the mosque, give them permission." According to another version, "Do not forbid women their share of the mosques if they ask you for permission." Bilaal – a son of 'Abd-Allaah ibn 'Umar – said, "By Allah, we will stop them." 'Abd-Allaah said to him, "I say 'The Messenger of Allah (peace and blessings of Allah be upon him) said…' and you say, 'We will stop them'?!" Both reports were narrated by Muslim. If the woman is uncovered and any part of her body is showing that it is forbidden for "strangers" (non mahrams) to see, or she is wearing perfume, then it is not permissible for her to go out of her house in this state, let alone go out to the mosque and pray there, because of the fitnah (temptation) involved. Allah says (interpretation of the meaning):

"And tell the believing women to lower their gaze (from looking at forbidden things), and protect their private parts (from illegal sexual acts) and not to show off their adornment except only that which is apparent (like both eyes for necessity to see the way, or outer palms of hands or one eye or dress like veil, gloves, head cover, apron), and to draw their veils all over Juyoobihinna (i.e. their bodies, faces, necks, and bosoms) and not to reveal their adornment except to their husbands…"

Then a second paragraph went on to explain, that the above texts clearly indicated that if the Muslim woman adhered to proper Islamic etiquette in her dress and avoided adorning herself in ways that would provoke fitnah, and affect those of weak faith, there was no reason why she should not pray in the mosque.

Half an hour later, Patricia covered her head in one of the modern, blinged-up with sequins, colourful designer *hijabs* her mother had bought her, for wearing when she chose to join Halkano in the women's quarters at the mosque for prayers sometimes. Halkano had also bought at the mall, new colourful *hijabs* and *bui buis*, though she didn't wear the full body cloak *bui bui* everyday nor cover her head all the time with a *hijab*.

Halkano had taught Patricia how to perform *wudū*, the ablution required before particular acts of worship that is ritual washing. They both purified themselves by washing specific parts of the body, to be able to pray and make the *niyya* that is the intention to do *wudū* and recited, *"Bismillāh i'r Rahmān i'r Rahīm"*. Patricia had learnt that this meant, '*In the Name of Allah, the Beneficent, the Merciful.*' Halkano had told Patricia that at *Madrassa*, the Quranic school, she'd always been taught that while doing *wudū*, they were glorifying Allah all the time, and the limbs of those who performed *wudū* would be shining on the Day of Judgement. She was also taught to remember that one cannot cheat Allah, for He alone is owner of Judgement Day. And that on that crucial day, the same hands and feet people have used for praying, will betray them and say what *Haram* they committed in their lifetimes, and so every person should strive to live the *Halal* way.

Now Patricia followed suit and washed her face and hands up to her elbows, then her head and feet to the ankles. The girls both scrubbed their hands, feet, face, nostrils, neck, ears, and arms three times.

"So, the next thing," Halkano held Patricia's right hand and slowly dipped it into the water, "is doing this three times."

She then pulled Patricia's hand back. They placed each hand and pulled it back, held it, and pulled it back, and then the other. Both girls then stood, bent, knelt on the prayer mats, and started praying as they touched their foreheads to the ground.

EPILOGUE

Halkano could not believe she was standing with her arms around Patricia, Vera, and Lucy – her new crew as they called their group of besties. They had all accompanied her to her new school, their former school. Three months before, she never would have thought it possible. Karen Preparatory School. Halkano still could not believe that the neat and awesome place was her new school. There was a huge swimming pool, and she had been told she had to learn how to swim. There were so many sports there, like hockey, basketball, and co-curricular clubs like Debate and Wildlife.

She turned to her friends and said, "I am going to have so much fun here. You know I was a Girl Guide in upper primary."

The three girls gasped.

"Halkii, you never told me that," Patricia said, pouting.

"Pattie, I thought I did! Before that I was a Brownie Cadet in lower primary. I'm so happy that here I will also learn swimming, and like Dr Bilal encouraged us, take piano lessons for I love to sing!" Halkano said and poked Patricia in the ribs to remove the scowl and pout from her face. They all giggled.

Patricia, Lucy, and Vera had all passed their KCPE well, and were soon proceeding to high school. Halkano, however, had to repeat Class Eight because she had missed her final exams when she got married off. She did not mind though, because she knew she would also pass her final exams at the end of the year with near perfect grades, and proceed to high school. She looked smart in her black blazer with gold trim at the collar and sleeves, white blouse, and short maroon and white checked skirt. Her hair had grown to the middle of her back, and was soft and shiny because they went to the salon twice a month to have their hair done. She got hers shampooed, conditioned, treated, and blow-dried while Pattie had her locks washed, moisturised, treated, and re-twisted. Their girl's day out at the salon also included mani-pedi as Patricia referred to it, at the nail boutique. Halkano had learnt mani-pedi was a shortened form and meant manicure and pedicure, which was having their nails and toes done. Sometimes Mrs Kwela joined them and had her eyebrows and hair done, and a massage at the spa.

Halkano had even added some weight. She stared at the row of personal lockers on one wall. The brass nameplate on hers spelled, HALKANO ABADUBA. What a wonderful new beginning. She was so grateful to her new best friend Patricia and her parents for coming to her rescue. Halkano was going to be a lawyer one day after all. She and Guyo were now staying with the Kwela's as their legal guardians, after the lawyers had finalised the paperwork. Each time Halkano remembered that her mother was in jail, a teardrop rolled down her cheeks. However, knowing that it was a step in the right direction as it would deter other parents from forcing their daughters to drop out of school, circumcising and marrying them off, always stopped more tears from falling. The most amazing part of this new journey was that the

Kwela's had promised Halkano, that they would pay for her to undergo reconstructive surgery at the Karen Hospital, to repair her damaged vagina where she had been circumcised. And that the specialist surgeon would repair the private parts of her body, which had forcefully been taken from her, including what she came to learn when she went to the surgeon at the hospital for an initial check-up, were the lips of her vagina called the labia majora and labia minora, and tip of her clitoris which had sensitive nerve endings. Halkano was impressed because she never thought that it was possible to do all that. She was also glad and happy, that she could now own her body and say aloud words like vagina and those describing her private parts; words that she could not utter out aloud before, even to Patricia and Doctor Bilal, when she was telling them about her circumcision, without feeling embarrassed. Halkano before didn't know how to describe what had happened to her. She just didn't have the vocabulary for it even in her mother-tongue, where rape in marriage was a taboo subject. But Counsellor Jane and Doctor Bilal helped her know the words to use, and to say out loud that she was raped. Now she and Patricia encouraged their friends in what they called #NoTeenShame, to own their bodies, and freely discuss adolescent sexuality and reproductive health issues.

A couple of days ago, the Kwelas held a birthday party for Halkano who turned fifteen. Halkano was so glad that Guyo had joined her at the Kwela's, in time for her party. Guyo was brought to Nairobi by two lady officers from Child Protection Services, which most people referred to as CPS. All the legal requirements had been finalised by CPS and lawyers from both sides. The Kwelas were now by law recognized as the guardians of both Halkano and her sister Guyo. Halkano recalled the conversation she'd had with her little sister, about their new living arrangement and why it had become so....

Halkano had found Guyo looking sad, seated on her bed with knees drawn up to her chest.

Chin between her knees.

"Guyo, what is it? Why do you look so unhappy?" Halkano asked

Tears sparkled at the corners of Guyo's eyes, but she kept quiet. After a short while she said,

"Halkii, why have we come to stay here? The children at school teased me and said Mama and Baba were going to jail! What did they do? Was it because of you? I heard Mama and Baba fighting before they were arrested by the police. Baba said you caused all this with your disobeying him, Halkii! Your bestie Misrat told me that you had gone far away."

"Guyo, do you remember the day by the well when I was crying, and you asked me why I was sad all the time?" Guyo nodded silently.

Halkano her voice fierce, said, "well, it was because Baba and Mama wanted me to drop out of school and get married! I refused but they pulled me out of school, had me circumcised, which is very bad and painful, and forced me to get married! And the man they took me to for marriage hurt me badly! I was in the hospital for a long time."

"I'm so sorry, sis! How did that bad person hurt you?" Guyo asked, her voice soft. The question was so unexpected that Halkano stared at her nine year-old sister, lost for words. She almost dropped the glass of fresh pineapple juice she had brought Guyo. A deep furrow creased Halkano's brow, and she busied herself by carefully placing the glass on the bedside table.

Finally, Halkano said, "Guyo, young girls like you and I should not get married, because our bodies and our minds are just not yet ready to do the grown-up stuff of women. That bad man hurt me when he made me his wife. And I had to be treated at the hospital. One day when you are a little bit older, you will get to understand this." Halkano sat on the bed beside Guyo and put her arm across her tiny hunched shoulders.

"Mama, Baba, and the man who hurt me will be in prison for a long time. That way, parents, guardians, and other adults will learn a lesson: to never force little girls out of school and marry them off to old men!" Halkano felt a surge of anger flood her body for having to explain all this to her small sister.

She continued, "Sis, what some parents do to their young daughters is evil. I went through a lot of pain and now that I'm healing, I'm working together with Patricia and her parents, Mr and Mrs Kwela, on a foundation that will help keep girls like us in school and safe."

Finally, Guyo straightened up, lowered her knees from her chest, and dangled them over the side of the bed. Eyes wide like marbles, with a big smile stretching her lips, her face looked radiant. She said, "so I will never go through what you did?"

"Yes, Sis! I promise that you just like me, are now protected by law. We are both very, very lucky to be taken in by the Kwelas. No one will ever hurt you. Here with the Kwelas, who are kind and supportive, you will go to the school I've joined, and continue with your education."

Guyo jumped on Halkano and hugged her in a tight embrace, "Good for you, sis!" Halkano held on too in the warm hug, tears prickling the back of her eyelids.

Later, Halkano's birthday rave was awesome and had started the previous night with a movie and game night at the Kwelas, and a slumber party for the girls and their friends. The day of the party had been so cool with a treasure hunt organized by Patricia in the estate, and many board games and others like Spin the Bottle and Never Have I Ever, which were all new to Halkano, though she had also taught her new friends, games from her community, like Tapha Ijolee, Arba, Nuura Kibbii, and Peelo.

The Kwelas had also already planned a beach vacation in Mombasa for the whole family, the coming December holidays, for Halkano and Guyo had never been down coast to the beach before.

Most important, Halkano was also glad that the foundation was now up and running, sensitising youth in Nairobi about sexual abuse and assault, under-age drinking, and drugs. She had also talked with Patricia and her parents about holding quarterly sensitisation trainings in Marsabit more so her village in North Horr, in collaboration with the Chief, the local community, the village elders, *Nyumba Kumi* elders and local organisations like churches and mosques. The trainings would highlight the need to put education first—especially equality on education for both girls and boys, and the need to rethink harmful cultural practises by adopting alternative rites of passage. Halkano's resolution was to fight for the girls in her community to have a right to un-interrupted education. The girls were also very happy that an unspoken crisis like rape was now being discussed openly in a youth program called #LetsTalkAboutThis, across the country. What a wonderful new beginning that was!

Halkano retrieved from her backpack the letter Galgalo had sent her and read it again...

Dear Halkii,

Sis, I hope you are well. I miss you and Guyo terribly! But I'm so happy for you and the new life you are leading. You are so brave and I am so very proud of you! Too bad that Mama and Baba had to go to jail in order for you and Guyo to be protected- but they deserve it! I'm sorry for the pain you went through at the hands of that evil man Sasura. I was broken-hearted that I couldn't help you. You have done well in highlighting the plight of young girls from our village, being forced to drop out of school by their parents and guardians and married off. What you went through, and the press and media around your case, has helped reduce child-marriages and teen marriages. No child should be forced to drop out of school. Your bravery has brought a change to our village. Some parents were happy selling their children; now thanks to you, this is no longer the case. Sis, please forgive Baba and Mama for doing this to you. That way, you will be able to focus on your studies and new life—and taking care of and encouraging Guyo, too. Laws and enforcement have been put in place in our village North Horr and across all of Marsabit County. Social protection outreach events have doubled so that girls and all children know their rights, and that child-marriage denies girls their right to education, good health and wellbeing, and ultimately a chance at being empowered. The girls will no longer listen when their parents tell them that the same man who will marry them will take them to school, for it is never the case. Many girls have now signed the pledge you did, are joining hands in shunning harmful rites, and are focusing on finishing primary school, joining high school and know they will be free to go to college or university, and further their education to help build a future for themselves. Just like you, they now believe that through education, they would be able to arm themselves with the ability to think, act and behave rationally and wisely.

Halkii, you have taught all of us that without an education, every child deserves a champion—one who will never give up on them, and you have become that person. So many girls now look up to up to you! You have made change possible. Your case is the one that has stirred the waters. I will always love you and pray for Allah's protection to be upon you. Always remember to recite Ayatul Kursi. In Madrassa remember our Ustaadh taught us that the recitation will calm you, for you ask Allah for help, to make your fear go away. Whenever you recite Ayatul Kursi, Allah will send down many angels to protect you. If you recite Ayatul Kursi every morning, you will be in the protection and safety of Allah all day long.

> *You have done good, sis; for yourself,*
> *Guyo, Misrat, Darartu, and all young girls*
> *who were at risk of dropping out of school*
> *and being married off. Well done and keep*
> *it up! Pass my love to Guyo. Tell her I miss*
> *her cheeky self so! When I go to visit Mama*
> *and Baba at the prison next month, I will*
> *pass your regards to them too.*
>
> *Love always,*
> *Your big brother*
> *Galgalo 'GG' Abaduba.*

Halkano folded the letter and put it back in her bag. She'd called GG and given him her email address, and because he had one too, that would be their means of communication apart from the weekly phone calls.

Halkano had also talked to Misrat her bestie on phone, and Madam Bullo too. They both confirmed that indeed as GG had told her in his letter, there were many positive changes at their village in North Horr, where schooling for girls was concerned, and how parents, guardians, the school boards, village Chief, and *Nyumba Kumi* elders, were liaising with the courts, police officers, coordinating with government agencies, and county administration, where social protection and social justice was concerned, to make sure no girl was forced to drop out of school, circumcised, and married off.

Halkano swore she would always be there for her community. Just like her Girl Guide motto, 'Be Prepared.' The Kwelas had promised to take Halkano to Nyeri in Central Kenya, where the guiding and scouting movement's legendary historic founder's Lord Baden Powell and Lady Olave Baden Powell, were buried. Halkano was so excited—

who would have believed that she would one day visit the graves of the Powell's?

Standing before her locker, Halkano did neatly the three-fingered salute and said from memory the Girl Guide promise, "*On my honor, I will try to serve God and my country, to help people at all times, and to live by the Girl Scout Law…*" and pledge, "*I will do my best to be honest and fair, friendly and helpful, considerate and caring, courageous and strong, and responsible for what I say and do, and to respect myself and others, respect authority, use resources wisely, make the world a better place and be a sister to every Girl Scout.*"

Halkano was happy with the awareness her case and Patricia's, had raised about rape culture, sexual abuse and assault, FGM, and child-marriages, for it was the only way for the atrocities to slowly but surely be shunned, and come to an end. More so, the issue of subjugated and at-risk girls will also no longer be the case, as they will be encouraged to finish school, reach for the stars, achieve their dreams, aspirations, and ambitions. Indeed as her teacher, Madam Bullo always told her, the sky is the lower limit.

-THE END-

Dedicated to the survivors of rape and sexual assault. We see you. We hear you.

GLOSSARY

Ama?—Informal speak "isn't that so?"

ADRs—Alternative Dispute Resolution. It is the settling of disputes without the involvement of a lawsuit, and judicial court process.

AK-47—An assault rifle.

Boma—Kiswahili for homestead.

Boda boda—Bicycle taxi.

Bakora—Kiswahili for walking stick.

Bangi—Kiswahili for weed/marijuana.

CCTV—Closed Circuit Television. A surveillance system that uses video cameras to convey the videos of movements recorded to a specified storage system.

DNA—Used in the story to refer to the test conducted to determine the genetic code of a person.

DPP—Director of Public Prosecutions. Refers to the office tasked with determining and overseeing prosecutions.

EACC—Ethics and Anti-Corruption commission. Office that gathers information on corruption.

FGM—Female genital mutilation. The ritual of cutting off, and removing parts of the female genitalia.

FM—Broadcasting method that utilises waves to carry audio signals, otherwise called frequency modulation.

Form ni ku-hustle—(the plan is to hustle) Kiswahili slang (Kiswahili incorporating English). Young people's informal talk referred to as Swanglish/Sheng.

GVRC—Gender Violence Recovery Centre

HIV—Human Immunodeficiency Virus. The virus that causes AIDS and weakens the body's ability to fight infections.

ID—Identity.

Ka- / Tu—Informal speak denoting small/inconsequential eg: "That *ka*-girl is accusing us of..." OR "That *tu*-boy is misbehaving..."

Kwani—Kiswahili and loosely transliterated to 'so what?' or 'really?' with sarcastic or sardonic connotations.

KCPE—Kenya Certificate of Primary education. The examination written by primary school finalists in Kenya.

Kesho—Kiswahili for tomorrow

Kiherehere / Kimbelembele—Kiswahili for referring to a know-it-all, rushing headlong.

KOT—Kenyans on Twitter. Refers to vocal people who use Twitter to discuss issues affecting society in Kenya.

Leo ni—Kiswahili for 'Today is'

IG—Instagram. A social networking service that is photo and video based.

IMAX—A cinema that uses high-resolution film formats and projects films onto large screen with steep seating arrangements.

IV—Intravenous tube. Inserted into the body to deliver fluids such as medicine, water or nourishments.

Juzi—Kiswahili for day before yesterday

Leso—The leso (Kiswahili) sometimes called kanga, is a brightly coloured, popular pure cotton cloth with a border around it, printed in bold designs with a

Kiswahili saying, proverb or expression inscribed at the bottom above the hem.

LMAO—Laughing My Ass Off. Used to indicate that something is very funny.

Nyumba Kumi elders—Nyumba Kumi is Kiswahili which means 'ten households' and is an initiative by the government, to encourage all neighbours within a vicinity of ten homes, to get to know one another as a sort of community policing, and also to enhance security and wellbeing.

Mvi—Kiswahili for white/grey hair on the elderly

NGO—Non-Governmental Organization.

Nairobi tuko rada—Kiswahili/Kenyan-speak slang meaning 'Nairobi we are alert/on the move/upwardly mobile'.

OB—Occurrence Book. A book where the police records cases reported.

OMG—Oh My God/Goodness/Gosh! Used to indicate that something is surprising.

Paroos—Sheng/Slang for parents/shortened form for parents (Pronounced '*Paruuz*')

P3—The Kenya Police Medical Examination form, which is provided free of charge at the police station. The form is used to show that a violent act was done to someone. It is a police medical report that acts as an exhibit in court.

PS—PlayStation. A video game console.

PTSD—Post Traumatic Stress Disorder. A disorder that revolves around the failure of recovery from a traumatising event or experience.

Rungus—Kiswahili for wooden clubs.

Si—informal speak denoting why not / eg: "*Si* you just tell us" OR "*Si* you just Shazam it"

Sema—Kiswahili for say.

Sawa—Kiswahili for okay.

Satoo—Slang/Sheng for Saturday

SGBV—Sexual and Gender-Based Violence. Acts done against a person's will but with relation to gender norms.

SMS—Short Message Service. Used for sending messages via mobile phones.

Tuk-tuk—Small three-wheeled scooter taxi.

TV—Television.

Uteo—Kiswahili for a reed tray.

Woisheee—Exclamation of sympathy

Wazungu—Kiswahili for white people / Those from Western-European countries.

Wi-Fi—A wireless technology for networking that provides high-speed internet and network connections.

WTH—What the Hell. To say that something is strange or to ask what is going on.

Yaani—A common Kiswahili expression / informal speak - "you mean..."